"I don't want to talk about that night."

Kadir stared her down. "Well, maybe I do. Maybe I want to relive it minute by minute."

Caitlin's face had drained of color and quickly she stared down at her freckled fingers, which were knotted together as if she were praying for divine intervention, before slowly lifting her gaze to his. And for a second, Kadir found himself lost in the sky-washed hue of those pale, Scottish eyes. How had he forgotten their quiet, blue beauty?

"Just tell me," she burst out at last. "Tell me why you're here."

Now it was Kadir's turn to pause. What *did* he want? To rewind the clock, perhaps? Would he prefer not to have participated in the passionate night that had followed, even though his actions had appalled him afterward? No. He did not want that, even if such a thing were possible—for how could he wish his son never to have been born?

"Why do you think I'm here?" he demanded. "Because I want to see him. *I want to see my son.*"

Sharon Kendrick once won a national writing competition by describing her ideal date: being flown to an exotic island by a gorgeous and powerful man. Little did she realize that she'd just wandered into her dream job! Today she writes for Harlequin, and her books feature often stubborn but always *to-die-for* heroes and the women who bring them to their knees. She believes that the best books are those you never want to end. Just like life...

Books by Sharon Kendrick

Harlequin Presents

The Italian's Christmas Housekeeper
Cinderella in the Sicilian's World

Conveniently Wed!

Bound to the Sicilian's Bed
The Greek's Bought Bride
His Contract Christmas Bride

One Night With Consequences

The Pregnant Kavakos Bride
The Italian's Christmas Secret
Crowned for the Sheikh's Baby

Secret Heirs of Billionaires

The Sheikh's Secret Baby

The Legendary Argentinian Billionaires

Bought Bride for the Argentinian
The Argentinian's Baby of Scandal

Visit the Author Profile page
at Harlequin.com for more titles.

Sharon Kendrick

THE SHEIKH'S ROYAL ANNOUNCEMENT

HARLEQUIN
PRESENTS

Recycling programs for this product may not exist in your area.

ISBN-13: 978-1-335-14873-5

The Sheikh's Royal Announcement

Harlequin Enterprises ULC
22 Adelaide St. West, 40th Floor
Toronto, Ontario M5H 4E3, Canada
www.Harlequin.com

Printed in U.S.A.

THE SHEIKH'S ROYAL
ANNOUNCEMENT

This book is dedicated to Clelia Accardi, who is a proud Sicilian with a great sense of humor. Clelia gave me invaluable help with my book *Cinderella in the Sicilian's World*. *Grazie mille!*

CHAPTER ONE

THE MOMENT CAITLIN walked into the room she could scent danger. It lingered like stale perfume in the fancy salon. It impregnated the plush velvets which covered the squashy chairs. A pulse of warning thudded at her temple because this wasn't the first time it had happened. The strange and indefinable feeling that somehow she was being *watched*—that alien eyes were following her. Several times lately she had found herself whirling around, expecting to see something or someone out of the ordinary behind her—but there had been nothing and afterwards Caitlin had scolded herself for being so jumpy.

Yet now her skin prickled with apprehension as she stood alone and looked around. At tall, mullioned windows, which gazed onto the wet bloom of an autumn garden currently bathed in soft light. She tugged at the sleeve of her home-knitted sweater and was grateful for her thick, woollen tights, which she'd worn because these big old Scottish hotels were always draughty, no matter how grand they might be. And this one was certainly grand, judging by its imposing exterior and soaring position over the city.

As instructed, she had arrived just before eleven and the clock was striking the hour as she was taken into what was obviously the most important room in the hotel by a polite manager with a curiously expressionless face. For the past ten minutes she had been waiting with increasing nervousness, wondering who on earth she was going to meet and what they were going to offer her.

A job, hopefully. Actually, 'the job of a lifetime', as the agency had excitedly informed her—offering the kind of salary which usually only featured in fairy tales. And if it had sounded too good to be true that hadn't been enough to deter her—because who was ever put off by something like *that*? Certainly not Caitlin, who had a hungry mouth to feed and nothing in the way of security for the future. Why wouldn't she explore every opportunity which came her way when opportunities were increasingly rare for a single mother who lived on a remote Scottish island?

She was just studying a rather depressing oil painting of a stag standing against a background of blurry purple heather when she heard the sound of a door being opened behind her. Pinning her most polite smile to her lips, Caitlin turned to greet her prospective employer—but the smile withered and died, like a dried-up leaf thrown onto the blaze of a bonfire, as she stared at a man behind whom the heavy doors were now being closed. She felt faint. Then dizzy. Then faint, all over again.

Kadir Al Marara.

It couldn't be him.

Please let it not be him.

But it was. Oh, it was. There could be no mistaking the aura of raw masculinity which radiated from the powerful figure who stood before her, owning every atom of the space around him. Caitlin felt the blood drain from her cheeks as she stared into a dark face which had haunted her dreams and her conscience for five long years, no matter how hard she had tried to keep it at bay. But the flesh-and-blood version of the man was even more disturbing than the image which crept into her mind when she was least expecting it. And one question circled round and round in her mind, like a dark spectre.

What was he doing here?

For a moment she couldn't move, so great was her shock at seeing him again. It was only when her heart had stopped missing every other beat that she allowed her gaze to travel over him—the man she'd never thought she'd see again. The man who looked like no other, with his darkly exotic good looks and imposing presence. His face was the most beautiful she'd ever seen, with eyes of glittering jet set in skin the colour of beaten gold. She reacquainted herself with his distinctive hawklike nose and the carved cheekbones which illustrated his noble lineage. And now she wondered how she could have been so trusting when she'd first met him. How could she have been taken in by his explanation that he was nothing but a businessman, when his royal pedigree shimmered from every atom of his impressive frame?

Did he *know*? she wondered. Did he realise he had a small son who was the spitting image of him? And if he did—what then? Was he going to storm into her life again and change it out of all recognition, as he had done once before?

Paralysing fear crept over her as she stood there, not knowing what to do or say, because Kadir's appearance was throwing her senses into disarray—and not just because it was so unexpected. Because he looked so…*different* from the man she had known for that brief snatch of time. His jet-black hair was obscured by a pure white *keffiyeh* headdress, which seemed only to emphasise the olive-hued beauty of his face. And he was wearing robes. Flowing robes of soft silk, which whispered against the hard contours of his muscular body. She half shook her head in confusion. What had happed to the elegant Italian suit? To the silk shirt and vibrant cobalt tie which he had slung with careless impatience to lie on the bedroom floor along with her discarded panties?

That had been his *disguise*, she reminded herself bitterly. Modern, western clothes worn to send out mixed messages, so that she—and probably countless other women like her—wouldn't be able to guess his true identity. If he had been dressed this way when she'd met him, would she have been so eager to fall into his arms and his bed? Caitlin wondered. But she would never know the answer to that. Their gazes had connected and a powerful mutual attraction had surged between them. And because of that, her life had changed for ever.

He hadn't told her he was a powerful desert king. There were plenty of things he hadn't told her. Things which would have filled her with horror if she'd been aware of them at the time. She had only found out about them afterwards, when she had tried to track him down. When she had discovered what a stupid fool she had been. And the power of that memory allowed her to suppress her fear and the nagging sense of guilt that she could have done this all so differently.

'Kadir,' she said, and somehow the word slipped from her lips as easily as breathing. It sounded almost calm—and so very different from the last time she'd said it, when it had shuddered from her lips in another cry of helpless passion. She licked her lips as a wave of nausea washed over her.

Because what if he *did* know? What if he had discovered the truth she had fought so hard to conceal? She thought about Cameron, safely at home with Morag, and, despite her thick sweater, Caitlin could feel another shiver begin to ripple over her skin and it took everything she knew to stop her teeth from chattering. Wasn't it her duty to discover Kadir's intentions before she even thought about telling him? Or maybe she was just dragging her feet, knowing that once she told him the truth, nothing would ever be the same again. She tried to keep her voice cool, as befitted a woman who had been deceived as badly as she had. 'What on earth are you doing here?'

Kadir didn't respond to Caitlin's question immediately, but then he didn't have to because he was King and could make people hang on to his every word. The most powerful king in the Middle East, or so it was said. He owned rich lands and lavish palaces, which many envied, as well as countless servants and trusted aides who would walk over burning coals to do his royal bidding. Why, up until a few short weeks ago, he would have agreed with those who commended him for his many attributes. For having his finger on the international pulse after all his hard-won battles to regain a lasting peace in his sometimes primitive homeland. To many, he had everything a king could possibly desire.

And yet...

He felt the flicker of heat on his skin.

Yet this woman had kept from him the most precious thing a man could possess. The fruit of his loins and rightful heir to the vast region over which he ruled. She had denied him four precious years of his son's life. Four years he could never get back.

And never had he felt such an all-consuming rage.

But he would not show it. He knew only too well that concealing emotion was the only sure way to triumph in this strange business they called life. Because emotion was just another word for weakness and it rendered a man as powerless as sexual desire. It could make him do things which were abhorrent to him. Things which could take your destiny hurtling towards an unwanted destination and that was a feeling he couldn't afford to have. Not ever again. Celibacy had made him strong and powerful—which was why he would ignore the soft gleam of sunshine which made Caitlin Fraser's hair look like a fall of bright flame. He would disregard her pale skin and gentle curves and the memories of what it felt like to be deep inside her, and on her, and next to her. He would forget the fact that once she had made him feel as strong and invincible as a lion. Instead, he would lay the bait and let her walk into her own, doomed trap…

'You seem surprised to see me, Caitlin,' he observed coolly.

She furrowed her freckled brow. 'That's something of an understatement. Of course I'm surprised. You disappeared without a word five years ago. You crept away in the middle of night and now you've turned up without any kind of warning,' she said and then added, as if the thought had only just occurred to her, 'How did you find me?'

He shrugged. 'Such tasks are not a problem.'

'For someone like you, you mean,' she accused.

Steadily, he met her gaze. 'Someone like me?'

'A desert king! A royal sheikh! Something you didn't bother telling me at the time!'

Kadir did not comment on her furious allegation. Instead, he continued to stare at her with that same unruffled curiosity. Let her condemn herself with her own words, he thought bitterly.

'I don't understand why you've just suddenly appeared like this,' she was saying. 'Is this some kind of set-up?'

'A set-up?' he questioned coldly, his fury growing as she continued to act the innocent and, oh, didn't she do it so well? Did women learn the art of deception in the cradle? he wondered bitterly. Might that explain why they were so damned good at it?

She nodded her bright head. 'I came here expecting to meet a prospective employer.'

'Someone you did not know?' he probed.

'That's right,' she agreed.

'Someone you did not know,' he repeated. 'And yet still you agreed to keep the appointment?'

Her soft lips opened in protest, as if she had correctly picked up on the censure in his voice. 'Well, yes. Why wouldn't I?'

'Even though it could have been anyone? Tell me, Caitlin, do you often arrange to meet up with strangers in hotel rooms?' His eyes narrowed with a sudden dark flare of contempt. 'Although I suppose you do have some kind of track record for that, don't you?'

Her pale cheeks flushed. 'I could say the same of you,' she returned. 'But this was no romantic rendezvous. This was supposed to be a business meeting and perfectly legitimate. It was arranged for me by an employment agency and I take every opportunity I can to find work because I happen to need the money.' She glared. 'Now that might be something which is so far off your own radar that you can't understand what it feels like, but I can assure you—it certainly isn't a crime.'

'No,' he gritted out, his voice growing harsh, and suddenly Kadir knew he couldn't play this game any longer—no matter how tempted he was to see how far she would go to conceal the truth from him. To count how many lies she told him before he wheedled it out of her at last. 'The crime is that you became pregnant with my child and didn't bother to tell me. That you bore my son four years ago without my knowledge—and I have missed out on every precious moment of his life ever since. That is quite some crime, Caitlin.'

Caitlin's heart was crashing so hard that it felt as if it might burst from her chest, but she forced herself to focus on the facts rather than the pain which was coursing through her. He *did* know! Of course he knew. Why *else* would he be here? He certainly hadn't thought twice about her since the night he'd seduced her with all that abundant charm, and crept out some time during the night while she'd been sleeping, without even bothering to say goodbye. She remembered waking up feeling dreamy and half in love until it had dawned on her that there was no sign of the man to whom she had given herself so wholeheartedly, other than the traces of his seed which had already dried on the bedsheets. It hadn't been until later, when she'd discovered she was carrying his baby, that she'd realised just why he'd been so eager to leave so surreptitiously.

Anger coursed through her in a bitter wave.

And that was what she needed to hang on to. The memory of his betrayal—and her own stupidity. The realisation that she had allowed history to repeat itself—and had allowed herself to be treated like a fool. But she also knew the bitter consequences which could befall women who buckled under the strain of a situation like this and she wasn't going to let that happen. Not to her and not to her son. She couldn't allow this powerful sheikh to just swan in and take control of her life, with that arrogant look of condemnation hardening his sculpted features every time he looked at her. She didn't need his approval. She needed to be strong. For Cameron's sake as much as her own.

Because hot on her anger came an even more debilitating wave of fear. A dark flicker of dread as she started worrying about what he was going to do about his discovery. And, more importantly, what he was *capable* of doing. About the worrying consequences of having kept this secret for so long. Because nobody else knew that the Sheikh of Xulhabi was the father of her son.

'I did try to contact you, Kadir. As soon as I knew I was carrying your baby, I attempted to track you down. At first I couldn't quite believe it when I discovered your true identity, but once I had got my head around it—I still continued with my search.' She shook her head and could feel the heavy sway of hair as it brushed against her neck. 'And believe me, it isn't easy for an unknown commoner to try to make contact with a powerful ruler of a foreign country. There are mechanisms in place to thwart you every step of the way.'

'But you *didn't* make contact with me, did you, Caitlin?' he accused. 'There were aides and ambassadors with whom you could have left a message, but no such message was received.'

'No. Because during my search I discovered what you had failed to tell me.' Briefly, Caitlin closed her eyes and when she opened them again she prayed that her face showed no traces of the terrible despair she had felt at the time. 'You had no r-right to sleep with me that night,' she continued, in a voice which wouldn't seem to stop trembling. 'Oh, I'm not just talking about the fact you didn't mention you were a royal sheikh and made out you were a commoner, because maybe that was some game you liked to play and you used to get off on it. Maybe it turned you on to deceive women in such a way.'

'You talk to *me* of deception?' he demanded witheringly.

'No. I'm talking about something else. Something much worse.' She sucked in a breath and it scorched at her throat like a blowtorch, her words taking her back to a place she rarely allowed herself to visit because it was still painful. Too painful to bear. The discovery of his deception had carried an even greater significance for Caitlin, for it had been like a dark echo from her own past. A reminder of just how easily men could cheat on women. She remembered the sense of foolishness and regret which had washed through her veins in a putrid flow— along with the realisation that, for all the blame she used to fling at her own mother, maybe she really wasn't that different after all. She had certainly been hoodwinked in exactly the same way.

'Because you were a married man, weren't you?' she accused, and now her voice was shaking with shame and anger and guilt. 'You had a wife back home at your palace in Xulhabi, but you didn't bother mentioning that on the night you spent with me, did you, Kadir Al Marara? Tell me, how many times did you break your marriage vows by having sex with other women?'

CHAPTER TWO

KADIR STARED AT the woman whose bitter words had just come hurtling through the air towards him like a swarm of bees, but they did not sting his flesh or cause him to flinch. Because any remorse he might have felt was diluted by the nature of her accusation and his mouth tightened with anger. She might have fared better if she had stuck to the facts. Why hadn't she just taken her share of the blame? Admitted that they had both been carried along on a wave of passion—their bodies taken over by a chemistry so powerful that it had been irresistible, even though he had done his damnedest and tried.

But instead she had played the guilt card and turned him into a stereotype of a man. The dark and brooding sheikh, like a character from one of those flickering black-and-white films he had once seen. And being categorised in such a way had happened much too often in the past for it not to have touched a raw nerve. How many times? she had asked him—and the answer to that question was just once, with her. But he would not give her the pleasure of knowing that—because might that not lead her to believe she meant something special to him?

'You begged me to have sex with you. *Begged* me,' he reiterated cruelly, and so great was his fury that he actually found himself enjoying her embarrassed flush of recognition. 'You know you did. Would you like me to remind you of the words you used, Caitlin?'

'No! I don't… I don't want to talk about that night.'

He stared her down. 'Well, maybe I do. Maybe I want to relive it minute by minute.'

Her face had drained of colour and quickly she stared down at her freckled fingers, which were knotted together as if she were praying for divine intervention, before slowly lifting her gaze to his. And for a second, Kadir found himself lost in the sky-washed hue of those pale, Scottish eyes. How had he forgotten their quiet blue beauty? The way they seemed able to look deep inside you, as if they could see into your troubled soul and offer it some kind of temporary solace. He had forgotten because he'd had no choice—because the possibility of how good she had made him feel had been incompatible with his life and his world. And he needed to forget it now.

Which was why he continued to stare at her,

without saying a word. Silence was a tactic which had always worked well for him in the past. If you allowed it to grow for long enough, the other person would always break it first. Because people didn't like silence. They were frightened of it. They didn't like listening to the noisy clatter of their own thoughts.

'Just tell me,' she burst out at last. 'Tell me why you're here.'

Now it was Kadir's turn to pause. What *did* he want? To rewind the clock, perhaps? To have carried on walking around the sweeping Scottish estate he'd been considering buying and not been distracted by her bright hair or the curve of her hips, or the darkening of her extraordinary eyes when she had turned around to look at him? Would he prefer not to have participated in the passionate night which had followed, even though his actions had afterwards appalled him? No. He did not want that, even if such a thing were possible—for how could he wish his son never to have been born?

'Why do you think I'm here?' he demanded. 'Because I want to see him. I want to see my son.'

She flinched, as if he had asked her for something impossible. He could see the moment of indecision which froze her slender frame, like a deer in the forest which had just discovered itself in the presence of the hunter. And then gradually, life seemed to flow back into her body and she shook her head a little, like somebody who had just awoken from a bad nightmare.

'Yes,' she said slowly. 'I suppose you do.' She reached down towards a green leather satchel the colour of a wine bottle, which she lifted with trembling fingers from the chair on which she must have placed it. Silently, Kadir watched as she withdrew a rather battered wallet and flicked behind a bank card, before drawing out a photo, which she handed to him. 'Here. Take this.'

He didn't look at it immediately. Just continued to fix his gaze on her. 'You think I will be satisfied with a picture?' he demanded witheringly.

'Won't it do for the time being, at least?'

Unable to hold back for a second longer, he swiped it from her fingers, taking great care not to make contact with her skin—as if he could not trust himself to touch her. And then he willed himself to stay strong and not give in to the sudden sense of despair which washed over him as he steeled himself to examine the first picture of his son. The aide who had discovered his existence had offered to get photographic evidence, but Kadir had stopped him because he had a deep loathing of the paparazzi and was loath to replicate their predatory behaviour. Information about the child's age and appearance had indicated that he was indeed the father, but it was instinct which made him certain and these days he trusted his instincts far more than he would looking at some snatched photo, taken from behind a tree.

Yet no amount of mental preparation could make him immune to the feelings which bombarded him as he stared down at a pair of jet-dark eyes so like his own. He walked over to the window, so that he could study it properly in the autumnal light. Judging from the bland background it was a formal shot, though the little boy's silky black hair flopped untidily over his forehead, as if no amount of careful brushing could tame it. Kadir narrowed his eyes as he noticed a tiny chip on one of the child's front teeth and a rush of indignation heated his blood. Had he fallen and hurt himself? he wondered. And why had nobody been there to protect him?

He turned away from the window to find Caitlin's eyes on him, the uncertainty of that blue gaze clearly seeking some kind of reassurance. And didn't it fill him with a vengeful amount of pleasure to discover that he wasn't going to provide her with any?

His lips flattened.

None at all.

'I want to see him in the flesh,' he clipped out. 'And as soon as possible.'

Caitlin nodded, her heart sinking as she heard his words, even though she'd been expecting him to say that. Of course she had. What else could he possibly say in the circumstances? Her heart twisted with a complex mixture of emotions, though she was ashamed of the one which was dominant. Which bubbled to the surface in a dark and angry tide and had nothing to do with her little boy but everything to do with *her*.

Jealousy.

Hot and black and potent.

'And what about your wife?' The words rushed from her lips and she could feel her cheeks flush. 'Will she want to see him, too?'

There was the briefest of pauses as his face darkened but his voice was devoid of emotion as he delivered his response.

'My wife is dead.'

And wasn't Caitlin appalled by the primitive rush of relief which flooded her body on receipt of these words? 'I'm sorry,' she said automatically.

'No, you're not.'

'I am sorry for every person's loss,' she defended truthfully. 'But mostly I'm sorry I ever slept with you, without knowing you were a married man!'

'That's history, Caitlin,' he ground out. 'I'm not concerned about the past. The present is what occupies me. I am not leaving here—and neither are you, by the way—until you have agreed a date for me to meet my boy.'

'Cameron,' she corrected automatically.

'Cameron,' Kadir repeated and Caitlin thought how his rich voice made the traditional Scottish name sound somehow exotic and distinguished.

And wasn't that one simple fact enough to make fear whisper through her body, as she acknowledged his power and might? Because not only did he *look* different from the man into whose arms she had fallen so willingly, he *sounded* different, too. Along with the flowing robes and headdress, he seemed to have acquired a steely patina, which made him seem distant and aloof. Influence radiated from every pore of his muscular body and instinct told her that he would take total control of the situation if she let him. So don't. State your terms, she told herself fiercely. Show him you won't be pushed around by anyone. She wasn't one of his subjects. She was a free and independent woman and, moreover, they were in *her* country.

'Of course you must meet, but I would like it to be on neutral territory,' she said, as it occurred to her that maybe she was ashamed of her little croft cottage. Scared how tiny it would look in contrast to his soaring palaces. Or was it because she couldn't bear the thought of Kadir's powerful presence stamping itself on her humble surroundings like a dark smash of stone? So that when he left—as leave he inevitably would—the place would somehow seem empty and diminished without him? 'How about here in Edinburgh? That would be as good a place as any.'

'I'm sure it would, but I'm afraid that doesn't fit

in with my schedule. I have to be in London this week,' he said coldly. 'You can meet me there.'

'London?' repeated Caitlin.

'There's no need to make it sound like Mars,' he purred. 'It's no great distance. Just over an hour by plane, in fact. My business interests are centred there and my time in your country is short.'

'It is?' she verified, unable to keep the hope from her voice.

'Indeed it is.' He inclined his head, almost cour-teously, as if he hadn't noticed her telltale slip of the tongue, but the flashing of his black eyes indicated that maybe he had. 'Bring Cameron to London. Is he familiar with the city?'

'No,' said Caitlin, acknowledging the humble limitations of Cameron's upbringing. He'd never even been out of Scotland before, let alone flown to London. But that had been deliberate. She'd wanted to shelter him from the world and from people. She'd wanted to protect him from the harsher side of life.

And hadn't there been part of her which had thought that if she hid herself away successfully, then a scenario like this would never have arisen? 'No, he's never been there.'

'Well, then, that's decided. I'm sure it will be an exciting destination for one so young, and there will be much to entertain him.' He flickered her a businesslike smile. 'I will arrange for my plane to collect you.'

Caitlin blinked. His *plane*? He had his own plane? Well, of course he did—could she really imagine the king of one of the wealthiest countries in the world standing in line with ordinary people at the airport? She licked lips which suddenly felt dry. 'It's very kind of you to offer,' she said stiffly. 'But I'm perfectly capable of getting to London under my own steam.'

His black gaze slanted over her sweater and, briefly, travelled down her knee-length tweed skirt, his lips curving slightly as he registered her woolly grey tights. 'But presumably not with any kind of style?' he offered cruelly.

His observation—actually it was more of a judgement—irritated her, even if it happened to be true. But Caitlin told herself it was better to be irritated than passive. He hadn't objected to her no-nonsense clothes last time around, had he? He'd been more concerned with removing them than providing some kind of fashion critique. But she wasn't going to start going down *that* road. It was going to be difficult enough negotiating the emotional minefield which lay ahead, without remembering how it had felt to lie in Kadir's arms while he rained sensual kisses all over her mouth.

'I believed I was coming here today for an interview about future photographic work,' she returned briskly. 'And as far as I was aware, holding a camera in often inclement weather requires practical rather than fancy clothing.' She hesitated. 'As for your proposed trip to London, I'd like to bring Morag along, if she can be persuaded to make the journey.'

He frowned. 'Who's Morag?'

'She's an ex-nurse who has known me since I was a child. She's retired now and helps look after Cameron when I'm working.'

'And how often does that happen?' he demanded. 'How often do you have to leave our son in the hands of this woman?'

It was a totally unfair accusation and the possessive note in his voice was more than a little worrying, but Caitlin told herself he was angry and people said all kinds of things when they were angry. Drawing in a deep breath, she met his hostile gaze with one of manufactured calm. 'I never leave him unless it's absolutely essential and I choose my work carefully. I don't take on jobs just for the sake of it, because I'm trying to grow my reputation. I do a lot of photographic work for an agency which is, I suppose, how you were successfully able to lure me to this hotel with the promise of a job. Which I'm guessing doesn't really exist.' She gave a bitter laugh. 'There is no job, is there, Kadir?'

The brief shake of his head gave her his answer, but as their gazes locked she saw the smoky flash of fire in the depths of his eyes, which his thick lashes couldn't quite conceal. Was she imagining the faint sigh which escaped his lips, which made her focus on them unwillingly, only to recall how it had felt to be kissed by him? And then a whole batch of memories came rushing back and there seemed to be nothing she could do to keep them at bay.

She wondered if he ever thought about the circumstances in which they'd met, when she'd been trying to capture the image of a golden eagle and he'd told her afterwards that he'd never been so mesmerised by a woman's neck. Or her bottom. Apparently, he'd been thinking of purchasing the vast Scottish estate she was in the process of photographing, though the sale had never happened. She'd often wondered if he might have gone ahead and bought it if he hadn't met her, or whether his infidelity had nudged his conscience and made him change his mind. Surely she was the last person he would ever want to bump into. She gave a bitter smile. Unless she was flattering herself by thinking she was his *only* extra-marital dalliance…

He gave a sudden click of his fingers, and that impatient gesture told her much more than words ever could. For the first time Caitlin caught a glimpse of the imperious sense of entitlement which marked him out from ordinary mortals and, again, she wondered how she could have ever believed he was a *commoner*.

'Of course there is no job,' he said coolly. 'Have Cameron ready to leave first thing tomorrow morning. One of my aides will arrive on the island to escort you both to Edinburgh.' There was a pause. 'And what will you tell him, Caitlin? How are you going to explain me to my son?'

'I haven't decided yet. I need to give it some thought.'

'Does he know who his father is?'

'No.' She shook her head. 'He's never asked.'

'Are you sure?'

'Yes! I swear to you.'

She heard a low hiss of air being expelled from his lungs.

'How can I believe you?' he demanded. 'Despite the hand you lay so convincingly over your heart!'

'Believe me or don't,' she bit back. 'But it's the truth!'

He studied her from between narrowed eyes. 'Come equipped for a stay of several nights.'

'Is that really necessary?'

His laugh was soft and low and taunting. 'Oh, Caitlin, can you really be that short-sighted? Do you think I'm prepared to be briefly slotted in to your schedule, like an unwanted dental appointment? That a few hours would be adequate for me to meet the child whose existence I have only just discovered?'

She hadn't given it any thought at all—it had

all happened so quickly that Caitlin felt as if she'd jumped onto a merry-go-round. Only now she was even more scared than before. Scared of Kadir's power and his potential to completely wreck her life, but equally scared of the way he could make her feel. Because why, after all this time, did she find herself reacting to him in a way which shouldn't be happening? Her body felt as if it were coming alive under that searing gaze, in a way it hadn't done since the last time he'd looked at her. It was as if her senses had lain dormant all this time—like the bulbs which lay beneath the unforgiving earth of winter before being brought to life by the first warm flush of spring.

He was staring at her with an arrogant air of propriety, yet righteous indignation was the last thing on her mind. She could feel the prickle of heat to her breasts and the low coil of hunger which was tightening deeply at her core. Flickers of awareness were twanging low in her belly and her throat felt desert-dry. She'd always had the artist's way of looking at the world—of seeing her surroundings in terms of light and shade and variants of colour. But now it felt as if she'd been wearing blinkers which had just been removed and, suddenly, her vision had become crystal-clear. And she found herself looking at Kadir Al Marara as if she had never really seen him before.

She noticed the faint shadow of new beard at

his jaw and found herself wondering how often he shaved. She didn't know. Just as she didn't know what he liked to eat for breakfast, or how he spent his days. She didn't know anything about his mother or his father and very little about his dead wife. His *wife*, she reminded herself bitterly. The woman he was married to when he slid your panties down before giving a low laugh of exultant pleasure as he discovered your molten heat. The memory filled her with shame—shame that she had done it and shame that it still had the power to turn her on.

This man is nothing but a stranger to me, she realised. I may have borne his child, but I don't *know* him. Just as he didn't know her. To him she was just a woman he'd bedded one night in a tiny Scottish town. A woman who had pressed her body close to his and murmured against his mouth, *'Please. Oh, please...'*

Shuddering with self-recrimination, she found herself wishing she could close her eyes and, when she opened them again, discover that this whole meeting had been nothing but a bad dream.

But that wouldn't be fair on Cameron, would it?

She couldn't keep hiding the truth about his father's past, no matter how much it suited her. She had been without a father during her own childhood and had been bitterly aware of the great gaping hole that had left in her life. Did she really wish the same for her child?

She wondered if her misgivings were showing on her face and if it was that which prompted the speculative look which Kadir iced at her.

'There's something else we need to discuss, Caitlin,' he added silkily. 'Just in case you were thinking of concocting some kind of disappearing act, I would strongly advise against it. Because not only would it be a complete waste of your time, it would also make me angry and that is never a good idea. And besides,' he finished, his voice dipping to a husky note so that it sounded like smoke on velvet, 'no matter where in the world you go with my son, be sure that I will seek you out and find you.'

CHAPTER THREE

CAITLIN'S PULSE WAS hammering as she fled the hotel for the ferry terminal to catch the boat taking her back to her tiny island home. Usually, on one of her rare trips to the city, she would treat herself to a detour. A little relaxation and luxury and a contrast to her very basic life on Cronarty. She would peer into the windows of the big, bright shops before treating herself to a hot chocolate with whipped cream and marshmallows floating on the top as she watched the tourists bustle by. But today her mind was so full and her heart so heavy that she couldn't face it. How could she possibly relax in the light of what she'd just learned? She needed to get home—and as quickly as possible.

On board the ferry she stared straight ahead, breathing in the cold, clean air in an attempt to calm herself. But nothing could stop the thoughts which rattled through her head as she saw the craggy peaks of Cronarty in the distance. She'd been born on this island. Been schooled here. She'd grown up watching her mother dream her foolish dreams, then watched as those dreams had been smashed—over and over again. As her mother had gone to pieces, Caitlin had internalised it all with the acquired bravado of the only child, refusing to show any pain, even when that pain had become unbearable. And although she had been glad to escape to the big city once the long battle had ended, Cronarty had been the only place she had thought of coming to when she'd discovered she was pregnant and alone. The island had felt safe, with its soaring clifftops and stunning beaches, against which the mighty, foam-capped waves of the Atlantic crashed.

But suddenly it didn't feel safe any more.

She shook her head, as if that might somehow dislodge the memory of the dark and brooding sheikh, but his image seemed to be firmly rooted in her mind.

Stepping off the ferry, Caitlin began to walk towards her tiny cottage, the chill wind whipping around her. Sometimes Morag brought Cameron to meet the boat if she'd been away but they wouldn't be expecting her back until later. What on earth was she going to *say* to them? How could she possibly explain to her sensible babysitter that her son's father was a powerful desert sheikh with whom she'd had a one-night stand? More importantly, how was she going to tell Cameron himself? She bit her lip. She hadn't lied to him. She *never* lied to him—

she'd answered any questions he put to her but there hadn't been many. He'd been too busy kicking a ball or swimming in the cold waters down by the bothy to pay much attention to his ancestors. Children on this remote place weren't into tablets or mobile phones. Why, she didn't even own a television set!

And Cronarty inspired its own particular form of loyalty—so that when Caitlin Fraser had returned to its shores, her belly huge and swollen with child, nobody had interrogated her about where the father was. In a way, living there was a bit like living in a capsule that time had forgotten. Cameron hadn't yet started school on the mainland, so his upbringing had been beautifully unspoiled. And yes, she was sure people occasionally wondered why the pale and fey Caitlin Fraser had a wee boy whose hair was as black as the night and whose skin possessed the deep gleam of polished gold. But they never asked.

And now?

Caitlin stared up at the sky, where heavy clouds as dark as iron were massing ominously on the horizon.

Now the outside world was about to burst in on their quiet little life like an unexpected explosion detonating the night sky. Her son was soon to discover that his father was one of the most powerful kings of the desert and tomorrow they were being flown to London so he could meet him. How did you even begin to frame something as monumental as that?

Guilt had riddled her heart for years whenever she'd thought about the lack of a father in Cameron's life—a guilt which had been quickly absolved by recalling Kadir's marital status and reminding herself that men were capable of great deception. Yet Kadir's wife was now dead. There no longer existed a reason why her son could legitimately be kept from his father. Not even her own sense of hurt at having been so badly deceived...

She shivered as she saw the outline of her home in the distance, but suddenly it wasn't her little cottage she was seeing, but an altogether different view. A treeless landscape, with distant hills. And a woman with her own dreams of becoming a successful photographer, whose life was about to be turned upside down.

She had been leaning on a five-bar gate, steadying her hand to get the perfect shot of the golden eagle circling overhead. The shot had been perfectly framed when an exotic voice of silk and smoke had disturbed her and the bird—which had swooped away out of focus. Caitlin had whirled round to remonstrate, but the words had died on her lips as she'd found herself staring at the owner of the voice.

Who wouldn't have been speechless if they were confronted by a man like Kadir Al Marara who had just appeared out of nowhere? A towering figure of a man, with jet-dark hair and skin the colour of burnished metal? Who stood out from the rusty browns of the Scottish landscape with the effortless dominance of a mighty mountain peak rising up in front of you? His black eyes had glittered with an expression she hadn't recognised, something she'd momentarily thought was haunted. It was only afterwards that she realised she had probably been right. He had studied her for a moment in silence, in a way which should have felt insolent but, instead, it had felt as if she had been waiting all her life for a man to look at her that way.

'I have disturbed you,' he had observed.

'Yes. You've frightened the eagle away.'

'It will return.' His voice had sounded assured, like no voice she'd ever heard before, and Caitlin had been fascinated by his exotic accent and the woven fabric of his words. When he'd spoken, it had sounded like poetry.

'Do you know about eagles, then?' she had asked him curiously.

The shrug of his shoulders had simply drawn attention to their power and Catlin had been so mesmerised by the play of muscles beneath his fine suit jacket that suddenly she hadn't cared whether or not he was an ornithological expert or that her perfect shot was now a distant memory.

'I know a great deal about falcons, for we have

many in my country, and all birds of prey share familiar traits.'

'What country is that?'

'Xulhabi.' Dark eyebrows had been raised.

'I've never heard of it.'

He had smiled again but this time the smile had been tinged with darkness. 'Few people have.'

It hadn't been the most conventional of beginnings, yet what had happened next had followed a time-honoured pattern—although it had certainly never happened to Caitlin before. The atmosphere between them had been electric. Off the scale. She'd wanted him to touch her. She'd longed to feel his lips on hers and the weave of his fingers through her hair. Even though she'd tried to tell herself it was wrong to feel that way towards a total stranger, she hadn't seemed able to walk away from him. She didn't remember what they'd talked about, only that it had felt like the best conversation of her life. At last, she had glanced at her watch, saying she really needed to be on her way, but he had seemed to share her reluctance to leave. And when she'd explained she was driving back to Edinburgh, he had offered to meet her halfway, for dinner. There was a place he'd known...

She'd known it, too. The food was famous and the views to die for. She remembered protesting that he couldn't possibly get a table at such short notice, but of course he had. He was a sheikh, wasn't he?

A fact he had neglected to tell her during the delicious meal they'd barely touched or the ecstatic night which had followed. But she remembered that when they'd found themselves in a softly lit bedroom, he'd seemed to have second thoughts. Suddenly, he had drawn back, with a stricken look on his face, which should have warned her.

'I should go,' he had ground out harshly.

She should have listened to him. She should have let him beat a hasty departure—but desire had made her into a creature she barely recognised. A creature which had been hungry and yearning and craving her first experience of sex. But it had been more than that. She had wanted to comfort him, too. Had wanted to wipe that tortured look from his face and replace it with a smile again.

'Please. Stay.' Her words had been little more than a whisper but his answering kiss had told her that his doubts had fled. She remembered the way he had undressed her. His slow exploration and her own wondering reaction as he had taken her to the stars and back. Why, it had been so easy between them that he hadn't even noticed she was a virgin.

'Caitlin! There you are!'

She'd been so lost in her thoughts that she almost jumped out of her skin as Morag appeared in front of her, her greeting splintering Caitlin's erotic introspection. But something was missing, because the childminder didn't have her precious charge with her…

Caitlin blinked in alarm. 'Where's Cameron?'

Had Morag detected the sudden panic in her voice—was that what prompted her perplexed frown? 'He's gone to play with little Rory MacIntosh today, remember?'

'Yes. Yes, of course. Silly of me. I don't know what I was thinking of.' Caitlin shunted out a sigh of relief but the concern hadn't left Morag's usually cheery face. And wasn't it an indication of her unsettled state that her first thought had been that Kadir must have somehow arrived here before her, to spirit Cameron away, right from under everyone's noses?

She looked at the kindly woman she'd known all her life and wondered how she was going to explain everything, knowing she needed to tell the ex-nurse the truth and nothing but the truth. She needed to tell *someone*.

'Have you got time for a cup of tea before you go?'

Briefly, Morag's eyes narrowed, before her face crinkled into a smile. 'Tea? I thought you'd never ask!'

'If you would like to follow me, Miss Fraser?'

Caitlin nodded as she trailed the Sheikh's aide through the huge and intimidating house, aware of Cameron's hand held tightly in hers. Her own heart was pounding with apprehension but she thought her son seemed more excited than nervous. Maybe that wasn't so surprising. It wasn't every day a four-year-old got to fly on a private jet. Or to travel in the chauffeur-driven limousine which had been waiting for them when they'd touched down in London. She'd thought he might have been overwhelmed by a bombardment of new and very luxurious experiences, but the little boy had seemed to take them all in his stride.

'Where are we going, Mummy?' he'd asked at one point and Caitlin had known this was the moment of truth.

Looking directly into jet-dark eyes, which were so achingly like his father's, she had swallowed the lump in her throat. Just keep it simple, Morag had advised her earlier, and Caitlin had clung on to the ex-nurse's words like a lifeline.

'We're going to meet your daddy, Cameron. Remember, I told you about him last night? He's come to England from a land a long way away so that he can see you.'

This information had been received with a wriggle of Cameron's shoulders—a gesture which had hinted at anticipation rather than suspicion and Caitlin had told herself she was glad. But she hadn't really been glad, had she? She had been afraid of so many things—some vague, some not. Because what if he was as blown away by his father as she had once been? What if he looked at her and found her dreary and poor and dull in comparison to his more dazzling parent?

And now they were here at Kadir's home—or, rather, one of his many international properties, as his aide, Makim, had coolly explained. Caitlin had received this particular piece of news with a sinking heart. She'd been hoping the meeting might take place in another hotel. She had wanted the reassurance of being on neutral territory, knowing that at any minute she could just walk out with her son and that nobody would be able to stop her. But the car had brought them to the most beautiful house she'd ever seen—tall and white and elegant, sitting on a prestigious edge of London's Regent's Park. In the extensive grounds she had spotted several stony-faced guards with suspicious-looking bulges in their suit jackets and walkie-talkies within easy reach. A couple of hungry-looking guard dogs had been patrolling the perimeter and she had successfully dissuaded Cameron from going up to pet them. It certainly wasn't the sort of place you could just walk away from.

She wished Morag were there to provide a little moral support, but the babysitter had been summoned away by a female servant and was currently in the kitchen drinking fresh mint tea.

'Mummy! Mummy, look!' exclaimed Cameron, letting go of her hand to point at a pair of stone cheetahs, which stood at either side of a huge set of ornate doors, as if they were guarding it. The two statues were gilded and their narrowed eyes glittered green, like real emeralds. Maybe they *were* emeralds, Caitlin thought faintly as Makim rapped on the doors, which were opened by a robed servant.

But she barely noticed the servant, she was too mesmerised by the man walking towards them, his eyes fixed intently on the small boy who was gazing around the stately salon in wonder. For a moment Cameron seemed too preoccupied by the vaulted ceilings, the jewelled chandeliers and mighty portraits of robed men on horses to notice anything else. But he must have gradually become aware that someone else was in the room and Caitlin witnessed the exact moment when it happened—the beginning of an instinctive love affair between her son and the father he had never met. And that knowledge was like a sharp blade to her heart.

She saw Cameron's eyes widen as Kadir walked towards him and the robed Sheikh crouched down so that his eyes were on a level with his child's. And, far from being disorientated by this exotically dressed stranger, Cameron just gazed back at him with all the bold curiosity of a child.

'Hello, Cameron,' said Kadir softly.

'Hello.' Cameron's voice didn't hold the slightest trace of shyness.

'Do you know who I am?'

'I think so.' There was a pause. 'My daddy?'

Kadir nodded. 'Indeed I am. And it is good to meet you at long last.'

He lifted his gaze to acknowledge the watching Caitlin and she felt another stab of apprehension as she met the fleeting look of anger in his eyes. She told herself it would soon pass and the best way to facilitate that was not to react to his rage—though her resolve was tested when Kadir rose to his feet and held his hand out to Cameron.

And Cameron took it.

'Shall I show you some of the pictures in the room and explain who they are?' the Sheikh was asking.

'Yes, please.'

It was astonishing—and Caitlin's lips flopped open. When it came to family, it had only ever been her and Cameron. He had never grown up in the bosom of a big, extended clan, with aunts and cousins and grandparents—perhaps that was what made him such a contained child. But there was no such containment now. He went to Kadir automatically and held up his hand to the Sheikh, who curled his olive-dark fingers around it. Almost jealously, Caitlin watched as they moved around the room in perfect symmetry, achingly aware of the physical similarities between them as they stopped in front of the largest portrait of all. Had she deliberately

blinded herself to the parallels between them, because it had been less painful that way?

'Do you see that man on the horse…the man
with the crown on his head? That is your great-
grandfather.'

'*Is* it?'

'Indeed it is. He was a very famous warrior and
also a great scholar. And you see those tall mountains behind him, with snow on them? They are the
high mountain ranges of Xulhabi, where sometimes
you can see snow leopards, if you are quiet enough
and look carefully enough.'

'Can *I* look for them?'

'I certainly hope so.'

'Kadir—'

Caitlin had opened her mouth to protest. She
wanted to tell him to tread carefully. Not to promise
things which might never happen and fill a small
boy's head with tales of snow leopards and war-
riors—but Kadir acted as if she hadn't spoken. As
if she had suddenly acquired invisibility.

'Tell me, Cameron, do you play chess?' he was
saying.

Cameron shook his head. 'I don't know what
that is!'

'It's a game. A game with kings and queens and
knights. It is a game of strategy and plotting—both
of which are very necessary if you wish to get on
in the world and which I will teach you.'

'Now?'

Kadir smiled. 'No, not now. Now I think it is time for you to have something to drink, for you must be thirsty after your long journey and we have a lot to do this afternoon.'

As if on cue—which Caitlin supposed it was— the double doors opened and a beautiful young woman appeared, with Morag following close behind, looking curiously unfazed by this unexpected turn of events. The moment Cameron spotted his childhood nanny, he gave a squeal of pleasure, running straight into her waiting arms as she scooped him up.

'Morag, Morag! I'm going to learn how to play chest!'

'Chess,' corrected Morag affectionately as she ruffled his hair.

'My daddy is going to teach me how to play!'

'Is he now?'

Morag looked across the room at Caitlin, a complicit look which obviously didn't escape Kadir's notice, for he drew his shoulders back and appeared to grow even more statuesque.

'Morag, why don't you and Cameron go with Armina?' he suggested evenly. 'I think she might have some Xulhabian candy for you to try with your drink. Have you ever eaten chocolate flavoured with rose petals and passionfruit?'

The sound of Cameron's whooped delight would

usually have warmed Caitlin's heart, but her abiding emotion was one of *vulnerability* as he went off with Morag without a backward glance, leaving her alone with the man she was terrified of being alone with, for all kinds of reasons.

Not just because he had bonded with his son with an ease she hadn't been expecting. Or because his interaction with Cameron had left her feeling strangely excluded. No, it was more basic than that. It was the discovery that she was far from immune to him, even after all this time.

She still wanted him. She still ached for him. Still lusted for his lips hard on hers and his arms tightly around her, making her feel as if she'd found a place she'd been searching for all her life.

Without doing a single thing, Kadir Al Marara was making her feel things she'd thought had died a long time ago.

Today he was wearing soft robes the colour of mercury—their bright, silvery hue contrasting with the darkness of his hair and making his eyes appear as impenetrable as a night without stars. Outwardly modest, the outfit covered his body from neck to foot, but no material in the world could have disguised the undeniable power of the muscular body which lay beneath. With an effort, she forced herself to meet his black eyes, though the faint spark she read in them suggested he was perfectly aware of what lay behind her silent scrutiny.

She cleared her throat. 'I thought the meeting went very well.'

'I thought so, too. Though perhaps you were hoping for a different outcome,' he mused. 'For Cameron to take an instant dislike to me and refuse to see me again, perhaps?'

She shook her head. 'Of course not.'

'Really?' His dark brows shot upwards. 'Wouldn't it be easier all round if that were the case?'

She wasn't going to argue with *that*—how could she, when just having him this close was sending her senses into a spin, so that she couldn't think straight? For a moment she stared down at the rug, trying to concentrate on the precise patterns of cobalt and claret. Knowing it was wrong to feel like this and trying like mad to put a brake on her emotions. But when she looked up again she encountered a steely gleam of comprehension in the depths of his black eyes.

'Yes,' he observed. 'Desire can be extremely inconvenient, can't it, Caitlin?'

Her heart was pounding so loudly she was surprised he couldn't hear it. 'I'm sorry?'

'Please. Do not insult my intelligence. I may not have seen you for five years but if I held a mirror up to your face, you would behold the expression of a woman who wants me to kiss her,' he concluded softly.

'How dare you?' she said.

'I dare because it is the truth,' he breathed, and now his black eyes had grown smoky. 'And what is the point in playing games? Be honest, Caitlin. If not with me, then at least with yourself.'

She shook her head and when she spoke, the words felt like rocks in her throat. 'You seem to hold the truth in very high regard, but only when it suits you. Did your wife know what was going on the night you slept with me, Kadir?' she croaked. 'Maybe you even discussed it with her afterwards and gave me marks out of ten. I don't know. I don't have much knowledge of this kind of thing, but did you have what some people call an open marriage?'

CHAPTER FOUR

KADIR FROZE, FOR her choked and wounded words hurt and he had not expected them to hurt. Because his night with her and its aftermath had been nothing like her bald accusation about having an open marriage. In fact, she was so far off the mark it was almost funny, except that this was no laughing matter. And although he had ignored her earlier allegations of infidelity because he'd been angry about having been kept in the dark about his son, he realised he was going to have to explain himself.

But it wasn't easy. Few people knew the truth about his late wife and there was very little on record—deliberately so. It had been hushed up by the palace both during and after her short and tragic life. Nobody would ever have dared ask the question which Caitlin Fraser had just asked and if they had, he would have shut down the conversation immediately, telling them it was none of their business and that nobody had the right to question the King.

Yet Caitlin *did* have the right. He could see that. She obviously perceived him as some kind of monster—perhaps with good reason, he conceded reluctantly—and that unsavoury character assessment could not be allowed to continue, not if his ambitions were to be realised. He needed her to revise her opinion of him but he must tread carefully if he wanted her to agree to his plan to allow Cameron to travel to Xulhabi.

Because that was the reason she was here today. The only reason.

'It's true that I was legally married when I had sex with you.'

'You'll have to do better than that, Kadir,' she said coldly. 'Surely all marriage is legal?'

He gestured towards one of the most comfortable chairs. 'Won't you sit down?'

'I'd prefer to stand.'

'Please,' he said obdurately, for her face had grown very white and he felt a flicker of concern for her welfare. But despite her initial refusal, she sank into the chair and he thought how out of place she looked in this lavish setting, in her well-worn clothes. Yet there was something so gloriously accessible about her, too—for she possessed a luminous quality which transcended the faded jeans and heather-coloured sweater. Was it that jog to his memory which made him recall a similar sweater, peeled off to reveal a thermal vest beneath and the rare sound of his own laughter as he had wondered aloud how long it would take him to reach her bare flesh. Hadn't he laughed more during those twelve hours than at any other time he could remember? He felt a sudden tension in his body as he acknowledged how seriously he had underestimated the earthy appeal of humour.

And perhaps Caitlin had sensed the unwanted erotic path of his thoughts. Perhaps that was why she suddenly thrust her chin forward with a look of pure challenge, her eyes flashing ice blue fire.

'I've asked you a straight question and I'd appreciate a straight answer,' she snapped. 'So please don't bother concocting any lies just to spare my feelings.'

Kadir began to pace the priceless Persian rug, the walls of the huge salon suddenly feeling as if they were closing in on him. How long since he had examined this particular subject? How long since he had wanted to, or dared to? He shook his head. 'It is difficult to know where to start—'

'I don't think it's difficult at all,' she said, her face taking on an intense expression, as if someone were digging a sharp object into her flesh but she was determined not to show how much it hurt. 'I thought we were talking about your *wife*. That's the woman you were married to on the night you had sex with me, in case you need me to jog your memory for you.'

Kadir recognised that he deserved her condemnation for what he had done, yet surely nobody could condemn him quite as ruthlessly as he had done himself. How many times had he woken in the middle of the night, plagued by the guilt of his actions—a guilt compounded by the realisation that he had been powerless to stop himself.

This woman alone had the power to override his will and his best intentions—and wasn't that an ongoing threat which he needed to guard himself against?

He cleared his throat. 'I think it's important you understand some of my background before I get to the subject of marriage.'

'In Scotland, that's what we'd call time-wasting.'

'I was brought up as the only child of the King in very turbulent times,' he continued roughly. 'As the sole heir to the throne, a strong sense of duty was instilled in me since birth. My destiny has hung heavy on my shoulders for as long as I can remember. It still does.' He paused. 'It is the tradition of Kings from the Al Marara bloodline to marry women of similar pedigree—'

'Like breeding racehorses, you mean?'

He shot her a look. 'Look, Caitlin, we aren't going to get very far if you continue to be obstructive.'

The tone of his voice was suddenly censorious and Caitlin suspected it would have intimidated many people. But she was way beyond intimidation. Way beyond anything she recognised as normal behaviour. Instinctively, she realised she was fighting for something—she just didn't know what it was.

'All right. Go on,' she said stonily, though she couldn't imagine ever wanting to hear a story unfold less than she did this one.

'My father had broken the mould of his ancestors, who had always married for duty. Instead, he married my mother for *love*.' He bit the word out like a curse. 'And paid a heavy price for it.'

'What do you mean?'

'I don't want to go into details about my parents' marriage, Caitlin. Suffice to say it wasn't a happy one and certainly not one I ever wanted to emulate. I saw this thing called love as nothing but a trap— and one which I was determined never to fall into.' He gave a bitter smile. 'So when the time came for me to take a bride, I was perfectly willing to wed the princess who had been selected for me by the palace elders. To accept that we had much in common by virtue of our upbringing and royal blood, and to enter into the marriage wholeheartedly.'

'And, was she beautiful?' she asked suddenly.

Kadir narrowed his eyes, for it struck him as a highly irrelevant question. Until he remembered his last sighting of his mother and the way plastic surgery had transformed her into a monster he barely recognised. And wasn't that what women were all about? he reminded himself bitterly. Shallowness and vanity, and a grotesque desire to stay young for ever?

'Yes, she was beautiful,' he said slowly, but felt no sympathy when Caitlin flinched.

You shouldn't have asked me, he thought. You should never ask a question if you are unable to cope with an answer you don't like.

'But for me, the most important thing was that she wanted to be a royal queen and to be my wife. She was eager to embrace all the challenges which came with that role. Or so she told me.'

His words tailed off and he would have given any amount of gold from his vast vaults not to have continued with this conversation. But Caitlin was looking at him expectantly, those wide blue eyes stirring yet another forbidden memory, and he forced himself to plough on with his sorry tale instead of recalling how soft she had felt in his arms. 'But the reality was that Adiya had no interest in ruling by my side. Nor in learning how to be a good wife and, in time, to produce children who could inherit my kingdom. She had but one interest...'

He couldn't bring himself to continue and shook his head, afraid that the words might choke him.

'Do you want to tell me what that is?' questioned Caitlin, breaking the fraught silence. Only now her voice contained some of the gentleness which had lured him in so willingly the first time he'd met her—and didn't that almost forgotten quality of sweetness tug painfully at his heart?

'And that interest was drugs,' he said baldly.

'Drugs? *Drugs?*' She stared at him at first with consternation and then with dismay. 'You mean—'

'I mean heroin, to be precise—although I understand she started off with cocaine,' he supplied bluntly. 'Don't look so shocked, Caitlin. Did you think the west had some kind of monopoly on addictive substances? Apparently, one of her cousins gave it to her to try and she liked it. A lot.'

'But didn't you… I mean, didn't you *notice* anything which might have made you suspicious, before you married her?' she questioned, seeming to have forgotten her antipathy towards him, at least for the time being.

'How could I?' he demanded. 'I had no experience of such things and our times together were limited because of *propriety*. Often she was veiled, her eyes downcast because of supposed *modesty*— at least that was my assumption, although afterwards I was to discover it was because the pupils of her eyes were like pinpoints and she wished to conceal that from me. Obviously, she was careful enough not to be really *high* during our chaperoned meetings before the marriage, but all such caution fled once the ceremony was over when I discovered I'd married a junkie.'

'Oh, Kadir,' she breathed. 'What on earth did you *do*?'

'What could I do? I wanted to help her, and for her to get better. I tried to ensure her supply was cut off, but somehow she always managed to get hold of more. I employed the finest addiction therapists in the world to treat her,' he added bitterly. 'But in order for someone to get better, they have to want to try. And Adiya didn't. She liked it too much. She liked lying around in a chemically induced state of bliss.' There was a pause and his words came out as a ragged whisper, as if the walls were listening. 'Until one day she overdosed, then lay in a deep coma until she died.'

For a few seconds, Caitlin felt as if she had been robbed of the ability to move, but it wasn't just that which made her feel as if her blood had turned to ice. Because Kadir's face had grown so ravaged that she wanted to get up and go to him. To put her arms around him and comfort him. But she was so shocked she didn't think she'd be able to get out of the chair and maybe that was a good thing, because it certainly wasn't her place to offer him solace at a time like this. Her mind was spilling over with questions she wasn't sure were wise to ask, but one was hovering like a dark spectre at the edge of a nightmare and refusing to be silenced.

'So when you…when we…when we had sex together,' she said haltingly, because she wasn't going to try to make it sound like something it wasn't, 'was she—?'

'Adiya was already in a coma, yes, and had been for some time,' he said harshly. 'She had no idea that I was breaking our marriage vows, although I knew, of course. And I...'

His words tailed off and the bitterness and self-recrimination which had darkened his face were hard to witness. And despite Caitlin's determination to remain impartial and not get sucked into some messy emotional quagmire, she couldn't seem to let the subject go.

'You should have told me,' she said, but she didn't tell him why. No need to explain that a lying and cheating man had provided the grim, grey backdrop to her own childhood—one twitch of its grimy fabric enough to send her mother into paroxysms of rage and regret. Because she and Kadir were not going to have the kind of relationship which invited unnecessary confidences of the type which revealed far too much of your vulnerability and inbuilt fears. 'If you'd told me I might have understood—and if I hadn't, then at least I might have felt as if my feelings had been taken into consideration, rather than you just ignoring them as if they were of no consequence. As it was, I felt second-best when I discovered the truth. As if I'd just been some vessel you had used to satisfy your lust.'

He didn't correct her. Had she wanted him to? She bit her lip. Yes, of course she had.

'Because only a very limited number of people knew about it,' he told her heatedly. 'Out of respect to Adiya's family we kept the illness completely under wraps. Even her death and subsequent burial weren't publicised, for the circumstances of her death would have carried with them too great a stigma for her family to bear, on top of her untimely death.' He paused, and when he spoke his voice sounded raw. 'And although I didn't tell you the whole story, I never made you any promises I would be unable to keep, did I, Caitlin?'

'You didn't tell me you were a king.'

'No, that's true—but was that relevant? It wasn't ever supposed to be anything other than a one-night stand—we agreed that at the time. It was supposed to be uncomplicated sex between two people. You even provided the condoms, if you remember.'

Caitlin's cheeks flushed, because hadn't that been another legacy from her own unhappy childhood? She had carried a pack of condoms in her purse since she was eighteen years old, because the thought of an unplanned pregnancy had been something she'd always feared and she was determined it would never happen to her. It had taken her another six years before she had opened that packet—maybe that was why they hadn't worked, maybe they had been out of date. She shifted awkwardly as she took her mind back to that night. What had Kadir said as his hand had slid between her thighs and he'd flicked a provocative finger against her molten heat?

'I can't offer you anything.'

No, he hadn't made any promises and now she understood why. But if he hadn't been able to offer her anything back then, what was he doing here now?

'So why did you come here?' she questioned. 'And why now? Why did you seek me out, Kadir?'

His eyes narrowed with unmistakable calculation. 'Can't you guess?' he said softly.

She shook her head. 'I'm not in the mood for guessing games.'

'I came for you because I have been fighting a war for the past two years and at times during that war, I was nearly beaten and broken and I lost... I lost much that was dear to me,' he husked. 'And sometimes, in the midst of the desert storms which raged around my troops, when my throat was raw and my body ached as if every bone I possessed had been snapped—I would think of you, Caitlin.'

'Me?' she verified, so surprised by his admission that she didn't stop to ask what it was he had lost.

'Yes, you.' He paused, his voice suddenly growing smoky as he began to walk over towards where she sat. 'I remembered how sweet and clean you had felt in my arms. I don't know how many lovers you'd had before me, but you made me feel as if I were the only one and, somehow, I could never quite forget that feeling.'

She stared at him askance as she took in the implication of his words. *How many lovers she'd had before him,* he had said, and the irony was that he had been the only one and he hadn't guessed. Not then and not now. She gave a wry smile. Maybe all that stuff about virgins being extra-tight was just the stuff of legend.

But the fact remained that he had come back because he wanted her—physically, at least. The watchfulness in his gaze had given way to a heated blaze, which Caitlin was discovering she was far from immune to, despite the shocking disclosure he had just made. Or had his bitter story made her want to offer him comfort of the most basic kind?

He was so close that she could see the pulse which flickered hectically at his temple and the way his lips had parted and it reminded her all too vividly of what she'd once had with him and still missed. No man before or since had ever made her feel the way that Kadir could and sometimes she thought that nobody ever could.

A sudden tension seemed to have descended on them, imprisoning them in a private and erotic world, and as Caitlin started to rise to her feet he reached out and pulled her into his arms. And she was so captivated by her own sense of longing that she let him. She looked up into the dark gleam of his eyes, unable to tear her hungry gaze away from them.

'I want to kiss you,' he murmured, his breath warm against her face. 'And you want that, too, don't you, Caitlin? You want it as badly as I do.'

It was a boast. A virile statement of fact, which couldn't be denied without inviting a charge of hypocrisy. And to her eternal shame Caitlin found herself whispering, *yes*—such a tiny word but one which managed to convey a broken note of yearning, which seemed to spiral up from somewhere deep inside her.

He framed her face with his hands and for a long moment just stared down at her. His eyes were like jet-dark lasers but his mouth was unsmiling as he moved closer still. As he lowered his head like a bird of prey Caitlin felt as if she were in rapid free fall, and when his lips touched hers, it was like landing in paradise all over again. A willing captive to the power of that kiss, she swayed as the Sheikh's tongue flicked into her mouth, tasting and exploring her as if he were determined to prove just how satisfying a kiss could be. And how ultimately frustrating.

Was that his intention? To kiss her for just long enough to make her respond. So that she would reach out her hands to anchor herself to him—encountering unfamiliar silk beneath her fingertips and realising how thin it was? She swallowed, rubbing at the hard flesh, his muscles so deliciously honed and powerful that she found herself longing to see him naked again. Yet despite her lack of experience, Caitlin could sense danger—only this time a much more subtle variety. She could feel her body starting to change and there was nothing she could seem to do to stop it. Her nipples were pushing urgently against the lacy scratch of her bra and that achingly familiar low coil of heat was beginning to unfurl deep inside her.

Was it the corresponding rush of desire which made her want to squirm her hips against his with unspoken invitation, as if she couldn't wait to feel him inside her again? Was that what prompted a soft murmur which was tinged with triumph? Caitlin swallowed as he smoothed his hands down over her undulating curves, as if he were reacquainting himself with her by touch alone. In just a few minutes it would be too late, because she recognised that he would go right ahead and do it to her. Here. Now. His finger was already straying to the button of her skirt. Another second and he would be skimming it down over her hips and pulling her panties down and…and…

No matter how much she ached for that to happen—she mustn't let it.

Because she was in jeopardy of reading too much into something which was purely carnal and she was much too vulnerable around Kadir, even after all this time. What chance would she have of standing up to him and fighting her corner if she submitted? How could she possibly safeguard her child if she was in thrall to the Sheikh and allowed him to weaken her with a single touch?

Her hands were trembling as she placed them over his powerful chest, tantalisingly aware of the thunder of his heart as she stepped away. Her own heart was racing so hard that she felt dizzy, particularly when she noticed the flare of frustration which backlit the ebony smoulder of his eyes. But she thought she could see something else, too. Was it surprise that she'd been able to resist him? She was pretty surprised herself.

Walking over to the window, she smoothed down her ruffled hair and adjusted her clothing before turning round to face him again, determined to keep her expression neutral.

'That's not going to happen,' she said.

'It very nearly did.' His black eyes glittered. 'You're surely not denying you wanted to?'

She shook her head. 'How could I? But want and need are two very different beasts, Kadir. I may have just fallen into your bed last time around, but there's too much at stake this time. We need...' She swallowed. 'We need to talk about the future. About what is best for Cameron—and I don't want any unnecessary complications.'

Her words filtered into Kadir's mind and he allowed himself to mull them over. A complication, was that how she saw him? As an obstacle or an impediment best avoided? Hadn't his mother thought exactly the same? He felt his blood turn cold but maybe it was easier this way. Easier to do what he needed to do. For all their sakes, but most of all for the sake of his child. Deliberately, he kept his next words casual and to most people they would have sounded like nothing more than an aside. But if any of his aides had been present they would have been instantly alerted to the anger which was simmering away inside him.

'I agree,' he said. 'The future is what matters now, not the past. I no longer wish to be a stranger to the child who shares my DNA and who will one day rule Xulhabi. Which means that Cameron will obviously need to spend time there.'

'You mean…in the holidays?'

'Not really. There is too much to be crammed into the odd week, here and there. He needs to understand his heritage and history, and be schooled in the many arts of kingship. I want to take my son back to Xulhabi with me, to introduce him to the land he will one day inherit.'

'Are you completely insane?' she breathed. 'Do you really think I'd let Cameron go anywhere with you until I've got to know you better?'

'Don't worry, Caitlin. I fully intend for you to

accompany him. And before you look at me with such horror in your eyes, what possible objections could you have? You don't have a nine-to-five job and even if you did, I could easily compensate for any time lost at work.'

She was shaking her head. 'Well, I can tell you right now that's not going to happen. At least, not yet—and certainly not now. This has been a lot for a little boy to take in. Can you imagine what would happen if we flew him out to the desert? He'd be completely overwhelmed.'

'I can imagine it all too well, yes—but I don't share your opinion. I think any young boy would enjoy the experience.'

She glared at him. 'Well, I think it would make him lose all track of what is normal.'

Should he tell her that Cameron's life was never going to be normal again? Kadir felt almost sorry for her as he made himself appear to consider her words. But he could read the fierce determination which blazed from her blue eyes and so he made himself go through the motion of shrugging. 'Very well. If those are your wishes, then I suppose I will be forced to comply.'

'They are,' she said, looking at him with suspicion—as if she couldn't quite believe he was agreeing so easily. 'We can start out slowly,' she added placatingly. 'Little by little, bit by bit. We'll get some dates in the diary. How does that sound?'

'Wonderful,' he said sardonically, reaching towards a bell to summon a servant. 'I shall leave you now to get ready for dinner. We will eat early so that Cameron can join us.'

'Dinner?' she echoed blankly.

'Of course.' Kadir felt a rush of pure pleasure as he registered the discomfiture on her face. 'You agreed to stay for a couple of days, didn't you? Surely you haven't forgotten?'

He could see her long neck quiver as she swallowed, before appearing to regain some of her customary fire. 'I'm not going to reconsider letting Cameron go to Xulhabi with you,' she warned. 'If that's what you're thinking.'

'Fortunately my thoughts are something you will never be privy to,' he answered smoothly. 'Though I cannot deny how disappointed I am that you have stubbornly refused to see the matter from my point of view.'

CHAPTER FIVE

'DO WE *HAVE* to go, Mummy?'

Caitlin gritted a smile which hopefully con-veyed a sense of calm she was far from feeling. 'Of course we do, darling. We'd only ever planned to stay in London for a couple of days, remember? And someone needs to get back to Scotland to feed your hamster!'

With fingers which were trying very hard not to tremble, Caitlin did up the final button of Cameron's brand-new coat, having to battle feel-ings of pride and resentment as the soft cashmere brushed against her skin. It suited him very well, as did all the other clothes Kadir had insisted on buying from one of the city's best-known stores—a bizarre shopping trip, by any stretch of the imagi-nation, mainly because they had shut the shop es-pecially for him. And although natural maternal pride made Caitlin acknowledge how cute her son looked in his new outfits, she'd been aware of feel-ing as if she had somehow failed him by bringing him up in such frugal circumstances. How she had blushed when one of the many fawning shop assistants had gingerly picked up Cameron's old anorak and questioned whether or not madam would be keeping it. Madam had declined, of course, though she'd been unable to rid herself of a stupid sense of disloyalty as she did so.

If only she could dislodge the uncomfortable feelings which were swirling around inside her, because this weird trip to London was making her realise that, physically at least, she was still in thrall to the father of her child. One touch from the arrogant Sheikh and she'd been all melting compliance. How weak was that? But you don't have to see him again for a while, she told herself fiercely—and there was nothing to stop her building up some kind of immunity to him.

Giving Cameron an encouraging smile, she ruffled his hair. 'The plane will be leaving soon and so we'd better go and find your…daddy to say goodbye.'

'I don't want to say goodbye!' Cameron shouted, in a tone she'd never heard him use before.

'It will only be for a little while,' came a velvety voice from the doorway and Caitlin looked up in alarm to see Kadir standing there, his quiet tone of reason worlds away from the look of fury he was flashing at her. How long had he been standing there? she wondered. Long enough to have heard Cameron cooing that this house was nice and warm? The implication being that the fire which blazed in their little sitting room in Cronarty never quite managed to eliminate all the icy drafts which whistled through the house in the dead of winter.

'Daddy! Daddy!' Cameron ran across the salon and hurled himself at the Sheikh, flinging his little arms around the legs of the golden-robed figure who laughed indulgently at his son.

And once again, Caitlin felt like the outsider. The usurper. The spoilsport who wouldn't allow what father and son both clearly wanted—for Cameron to accompany the Sheikh to Xulhabi. She had been forced to listen while Kadir had waxed lyrical about his land. His poetic words had created vivid images of the country's capital city of Azraq, where apparently a pair of red-footed falcons—the rarest of all the falcons—lived amid the soaring golden towers of the palace. He had regaled Cameron with tales of horse-riding and archery and how, when he was just seven years old, he had learned to sword-fight.

'Can *I* learn to sword-fight, Daddy?' Cameron had asked plaintively and Caitlin's natural fears had made her wonder aloud about danger, before Kadir had given her a withering look, which had scorched across the room over his son's dark head.

'You think I would put him in *danger*?' he had demanded. 'Don't you realise that in some countries boys learn to sword-fight as young as five?'

'Not in Scotland, they don't!'

'Then all I can say is—it's a pity for Scotland!'

And that was how it had gone on. Their two-day stay in the Sheikh's luxury home had been difficult, to say the least—well, for her anyway. Not for Cameron, that was for sure. He had been happy enough to participate in the dizzying array of treats which had been planned for him and had quickly adapted to the bizarre concept of discovering that his previously unknown father was a powerful king of the desert.

Maybe children weren't as aware of status as adults were, she thought. Cameron hadn't commented on the fact that Kadir's house was so big you could have fitted ten of their tiny cottages into its extensive space. Or that countless servants could constantly be seen gliding past, or silently lurking in corners—always ready to do the Sheikh's bidding. And he certainly hadn't raised any objections when they were whisked around London in yet another fancy car, with a professional guide who had been hired for their stay. Though in truth she thought that Kadir could have qualified for guide status himself, he seemed to know so much about the city.

'Xulhabi does a lot of trade with the world's major cities—so naturally I make it my business to know as much about them as possible,' he had replied, in answer to Morag's question. But he had followed this up with a smile which had made the middle-aged nanny melt—as usual. A smile which was also doled out on regular occasions to Cameron.

But never to her.

For her he reserved his best icy expression— a look as chilly as the wild winds which howled around the shores of Cronarty. Was he still angry that she had refused to allow Cameron to go back to Xulhabi with him, when surely he must realise that her reasons were perfectly valid? Or were they?

Weren't they based on fear? A nebulous fear she couldn't quite grasp and certainly couldn't articulate?

It had been a shock to find out about his late wife's drug addiction and her subsequent coma, but in a way it had added to the confusion of her feelings. The reasons for his infidelity no longer seemed so black and white, but that didn't change the fact that he had kept his identity and marital status secret from her. She just needed some time alone to make sense of all she had learned and then to come to some acceptable decision about their future.

Standing beside their small suitcase, Caitlin waited patiently while Cameron said his final goodbyes, but she could do nothing about the twist in her heart as the Sheikh gently disengaged Cameron's arms and crouched down to look deep into his son's eyes.

'We will see each other again very soon, my boy,' he said gently. 'I promise.'

Cameron nodded fiercely and before Caitlin knew it, the limousine was outside waiting and ready to go.

She was quiet during the journey to the airfield, where the plane was waiting to take them back to Edinburgh—and the fact that the aircraft was much bigger and shinier than the one they'd flown in before obviously cheered Cameron up. But Caitlin's heart remained heavy as they were taken through to a roomy cabin at the back of the aircraft and told to make themselves comfortable. Busying herself, she buckled up her son's seat belt, then watched as he gazed through the window at the thick clouds outside.

As the engines began to power into life, she turned to Morag, needing some kind of reassurance. Wanting someone to tell her that everything was going to be okay—because why was some inexplicable sinking sensation in her stomach making her feel strangely *doomed*? 'That didn't go so badly,' she observed quietly, more in an effort to convince herself. 'Considering how difficult it *might* have been.'

'No. Not bad at all. I like him,' Morag added, and then, after a pause, her brogue grew very gruff. 'I like him a lot.'

Caitlin wondered if she was imagining the faint

reprimand behind the nanny's praise, or was that just her own paranoia getting the better of her? A childish urge to grit out a litany of complaints about the Sheikh was making her face feel hot and flushed, but she suspected that Morag would have no truck with her objections. Why, she'd even been understanding when Caitlin had briefly explained that Kadir's wife had been in a coma for most of their short marriage, though she didn't explain why. If she had been expecting the middle-aged nanny to make a negative judgement about his illicit night with her, then she was destined to be disappointed.

'Poor man,' had been Morag's only comment.

Poor man? What about *her*? Caitlin had wanted to ask. Didn't her feelings come into it? Didn't Morag realise how difficult it was going to be to adapt their lives in the light of the Sheikh's dramatic reappearance? Already she was fretting about how many days of the year Kadir would expect to see his son.

But Morag's words forced Caitlin to take a step back and try to look at the matter from a different perspective. It had made her realise that Kadir was not all bad, just as she was not all good. And that insight didn't sit particularly comfortably with her. As soon as she got back to the island, she resolved to contact him. She would tell him that they needed to work out—in as civilised a way as possible— a timetable for future meetings. She needed to get past her own feeling of having been duped by his omission to tell her about his marital status. She had to move on from the way it had made her feel when she'd discovered it. They all did.

Yet still her nagging feeling of disquiet wouldn't shift. The plane provided every conceivable luxury and they were offered delicious drinks, fruit and pastries—but although Cameron and Morag tucked in with alacrity, Caitlin had no appetite for hers. Instead, she found her gaze wandering around the cabin, noticing the exquisite surroundings of the royal aircraft. It was fitted out with sandalwood furniture adorned with Xulhabian insignia and featuring those two striking sitting cheetahs.

A glossy US magazine was lying on one of the tables with the Sheikh's stark image dominating the cover and Caitlin could do nothing about the sudden leap of her heart as she picked it up. Enigmatic and darkly regal, Kadir was wearing a traditional white garment, and on his arm sat a falcon—its beady eyes gleaming with faint menace at the camera. Caitlin flicked through the pages and started reading the article, which heaped praise on the 'notoriously private' ruler's attempts to establish a peaceful state in the desert region after so much warfare. It spoke of his fierceness and his bravery in battle. It was hard not to be impressed and she didn't want to be impressed. In an attempt to distract herself from the glowing accounts of his dip-

lomatic triumphs, she found herself studying a map
of Xulhabi, and realising for the first time just how
big a country it was. What must it be like to be King
of such a place? she wondered. To have grown up
knowing that, one day, all that would be yours—
along with the weight of responsibility which came
with such a role.

*And Kadir expected Cameron to share that
weight! For a boy of not yet five, surely that was
too great a burden for him to have to carry?*

They were over an hour into the flight before
Caitlin began to sense that something was wrong
and it all began with a polite enquiry made to one
of the beautiful Xulhabian stewardesses, whose response was mystifying. Did she *really* not understand a simple question about what time they were
expected to land in Edinburgh? Instead, the woman
flashed a non-committal smile before scuttling off
towards the front of the plane and Caitlin was left
feeling perplexed. Moments later she glanced out
of the cabin window to discover that now the clouds
had cleared, her view was unimpeded, but instead
of the russet tones and undulating views of Scotland, she could see…

She remembered a long-ago holiday before her
son had been born and her breathless wonder as she
had gazed out of the cabin window.

She closed her eyes as if to convince herself that
her vision must be playing tricks on her, but when

she opened them again, the scene outside was exactly the same.

She told herself not to be so stupid. Of *course* those snow-capped mountains weren't the dominating peaks of the Alps. How *could* they be?

But it was funny how you could convince yourself something wasn't true even when you knew it was. She allowed another fifteen minutes to pass, but the stunning vista below them showed no sign of magically giving way to the much lower peaks of home.

Caitlin felt dizzy.

Sick.

She wanted to blurt out her fears to someone—anyone—but Morag was busily doing some colouring with Cameron and she didn't want to alarm him. Besides, what if her fears were unwarranted? What if...?

But you wouldn't need to be an aviation expert to realise that they were way off course and Caitlin rose unsteadily to her feet. Walking to the front of the plane, she found the stewardess in a cabin almost as large as the one in which she'd left Cameron and Morag. Her head had been so full that she hadn't really noticed it while passing through at the beginning of the journey, but now she became aware that this area of the plane was almost palatial. It boasted rich velvet sofas and lacquered lamps. And a very old writing desk on which sat a beautiful emerald and silver paper knife, which was fashioned to look like a dagger.

'Could you please tell me what's going on?' Caitlin said, her crisp question belying the growing dread at the base of her stomach.

The stewardess's stunning eyes became shuttered. 'Going on?' she echoed.

Caitlin bristled because it was adding insult to injury to have the woman treat her as if she were some kind of idiot. 'I know we're flying off course,' she accused, keeping her voice deliberately low. 'And I'd like an explanation of just what is happening!'

'I'm afraid I cannot—'

'It's okay, Rania. You can leave us now.'

The velvety voice from behind them could have come from only one source and Caitlin whirled round—shock and fury washing over her, along with something else. Something powerful and all-consuming. Something which felt uncomfortably like desire as her disbelieving gaze took in the dominating figure who was standing in the doorway.

Kadir Al Marara, all-powerful and muscular, his hawklike features enigmatic.

Only his black eyes moved—for they were watchful and glittering as they raked over her. Suddenly Caitlin was reminded of the falcon she'd seen on the magazine cover—dark and still and potentially deadly—and a whisper of foreboding shivered over her skin as she returned his hooded gaze.

She was vaguely aware of Rania exiting the salon as fast as her high-heeled shoes would allow, leaving her alone with him, and her heart thumped painfully against her ribcage as she tried to make some sense out of what she was seeing.

'I don't understand,' she said. 'What are you doing here?'

He shrugged. 'Up until a few moments ago, I was flying the plane.'

His deliberate misunderstanding of her question tipped the temper she hadn't even realised she'd been holding in check and the words suddenly exploded from Caitlin's lips. 'I'm not interested in your piloting skills!' she hissed, clenching her fists by her sides as she experienced an overwhelming desire to pummel them hard against his powerful chest. 'I'd like to know why we haven't landed in Scotland.'

'Because we aren't flying to Scotland.'

'Yes, we are! You know we are! That's what we agreed!' she babbled stupidly and then her voice rose. 'Where are you taking us?'

'You know exactly where I'm taking you, Caitlin,' he informed her silkily. 'To Xulhabi.'

'You can't,' she said, her voice dropping to a disbelieving whisper. 'You can't do that. That's… that's *kidnap*!'

Kadir stared at her, steeling himself against the suddenly vulnerable tremble of her lips and the widening of her sky-washed eyes. 'That's one way of looking at it, I suppose,' he drawled. 'I would prefer to think of it as purposefully reuniting with my family.'

'How dare you?'

'I dare because I have no choice,' he told her simply. 'I owe it, not only to my people, but also to my son—to allow him to set foot on the soil of his forebears. And he cannot do that if his mother is proving unreasonably resistant, and he is stuck on some remote island far away, unable to access the skills he will require when he rules Xulhabi.'

'Will you stop saying that?' she demanded. 'You make it sound as if it's a done deal, when Cameron might not want to be the heir to your wretched country! He might want to be a…a farmer—or a vet!'

'I'm afraid that's not going to happen, Caitlin,' he replied, with a steely air of finality. 'It cannot happen. His destiny is ordained.'

She gasped as the import of his words must have dawned on her—because suddenly she was launching herself at him like a wildcat, all that vulnerability vanished as she began to pummel her fists urgently against his chest.

'Caitlin—that isn't going to do you any good,' he protested, though without the kind of conviction he might have expected. Because wasn't there a part of him which was actively *enjoying* her anger and her outrage? Wasn't the heavy throb of his erection an inevitable response to having her this close to him again and breathing in her particular scent, which made him think of soap and honey and wild Scottish moors? A sudden wild rush of yearning pulsed through him and he longed to tangle his fingers in the bright banner of her hair, but he forced himself to ignore it and confront the problem in hand. 'Stop it.'

'No! I won't stop it!' she declared, with another blow to his chest, which he barely felt, even though she was obviously putting all her weight behind it. 'Not until you direct the pilot—or do it yourself— to turn this wretched plane right round and take us to Edinburgh!'

'Sorry,' he said, with an adamant shake of his head. 'I can't do that.'

Did his words suddenly take root or did she just realise that he meant them? Was that why she stopped her rhythmic pummelling so he thought she might have ceased her attack? But, no, his guess was way off mark—or maybe he had underestimated her. For she was swooping towards the writing desk with all the force of a heat-seeking missile. And, moments later, she was back, brandishing the jewelled paper knife above him.

'Take me back home immediately, or I'll scar that beautiful face of yours!' she declared.

He wanted to kiss her. He wanted that so badly. And, judging by the hungry look which suddenly flashed from her eyes, so did she. As he caught hold of the wrist of the hand which held the jewelled dagger he could feel her tremble with something which didn't feel remotely like fear—and the instinctive parting of her lips was as powerful an invitation to kiss her as he'd ever seen. Though what did *he* know of a woman's true desires?

Kadir couldn't deny that the temptation was as powerful as any he had ever experienced, but he resisted it as he had done so many times before. Because this wasn't about sex. It was about power. His power—and hers, too. He wondered if she understood that she was in the rare position of having something he wanted. Something he hadn't been expecting to find—and which felt like the most precious gift he'd ever been presented with.

His son.

Within the veins of his child ran the true blue blood of a future king and nothing could change that unassailable fact—not Caitlin's wishes, nor his own. After so many years of warfare and disruption, the royal line of Xulhabi was more important than any one person's personal desire or agenda. It was his duty to provide an heir for his people and now it was within his ability to do so. Only Caitlin Fraser stood in his way.

Kadir knew he couldn't afford to let Cameron out of his sight for a moment because he didn't trust her. And why should he when she had seemed so eager to block all his attempts to get to know his son better? When she had spoken so primly and parsimoniously about getting *'some dates in the diary'*. As if she were some middle-aged matron scheduling in a dinner party! For all he knew, she might take it upon herself to 'disappear'—and, although he had the resources to find her, to play a cat-and-mouse game while he hunted her down would be disruptive and unpleasant for everyone concerned. Especially Cameron.

'Drop the knife, Caitlin,' he said silkily.

'I *won't*!' She wriggled within his grasp. 'Not until you agree to turn this plane round and fly us back home.'

'Drop the knife,' he repeated, trying to ignore the insistent throb of his erection and the even more insistent desire to crush his lips down over the soft quiver of her own and lose himself in her kiss. 'Drop it right now, or I shall be forced to have one of the palace doctors meet us when we land and declare you mentally unsound to care for our son.'

His words must have hit home for her grip loosened and the sound of the knife bouncing off the polished wooden floor sounded deafening as she stared up at him, her mulish expression now tinged with wariness. 'You wouldn't dare?'

'Oh, I would. I would stop at nothing to get my way on this. Believe me when I tell you that—even if that is the last thing I want to do. Because you are testing my patience just a little too far.'

'You're a fine one to talk about testing patience!' she flashed back. 'Think about it! It's not just me and Cameron you're strong-arming back to your country—there's Morag, too, over whom you have no power at all! What has she done to deserve all this? Don't you think that the first opportunity she gets, she'll be on the phone to the Foreign Office telling them what you've done and demanding they get us back home as soon as possible? And they'll come after you—you can bet your sweet life they will! The British government will lock you up and throw away the key. Hopefully for ever! Because kidnap is kidnap—no matter how high-born and mighty you are!'

'Your imagination is remarkably vivid but essentially flawed—since I suspect you might find that Morag's sympathies are very much in tune with my dilemma. She has certainly been very accommodating thus far,' he mused. 'Which begs the question: Can't you do the same—at least for the time being? Don't alarm our son by an unnecessary display of hysteria, Caitlin. Accept the situation for what it is and try to make the best of it.'

'How can I possibly do that?' she demanded. 'When I don't know even what "the situation" is!'

'But you will. In time,' he said smoothly. 'There are many issues we need to address about the future and they will be discussed in more detail when we arrive at my royal palace.'

She stared at him. 'So I don't really have a choice, do I?'

He shook his head. 'No, Caitlin. I'm afraid you don't.'

CHAPTER SIX

'YOU ARE PALE, CAITLIN.'

'Of course I'm pale! I've just had a severe life shock! I wasn't expecting to be hijacked while I was in the air and then flown to some wretched hellhole of a place against my will!'

'I would not describe the royal palace of Xulhabi as a hellhole and we are not going to conduct this conversation in an inflammatory manner, if that's what you're hoping.'

Kadir's voice was as soft as the warm air which scented the courtyard—the rustle of his robes the only sound Caitlin could hear above the distant tinkling of a fountain. Outside the sky was the most beautiful she'd ever seen, a deep indigo canopy punctured by stars so bright, it almost dazzled the eye to gaze upon them. But gaze on them she did, because anything was better than having to look Kadir in the eye and try to pretend that he wasn't making her pulse-rate soar with anger, outrage and that annoying ever-present throb of desire.

She needed to concentrate on what he had actually *done*, which was an affront, by anyone's standards. And didn't his high-handedness and outrageous flexing of power cancel out a little of the understanding she'd been starting to feel towards him?

'What I'm hoping,' she spat out, 'is that you see sense. That you'll understand you can't just go around *kidnapping* people like some *despot*. If you let the three of us go home, before any irretrievable damage is done, then we'll just draw a line in the sand and move on.'

'I think you need to compose yourself,' he said, with infuriating calm. 'Did you like the clothes which I arranged to have sent to your suite?'

Caitlin wished he wouldn't try to change the subject, especially one which was difficult to answer without sounding *grateful*. Yet how could she fail to like the delicate tunics she'd found neatly lined up in one of the wardrobes? In rainbow colours, the fabrics were so fine that they felt like a cloud to the touch. As a gesture of defiance she had wanted to ignore the whole lot of them and just dress normally—but, despite the palace's super-efficient air-conditioning, she couldn't possibly wear her trademark sweater and sensible tweed skirt in this hot climate. So she had reluctantly slipped on one of the tunics while silently despairing at the way it managed to make her feel so ethereal and so...*feminine*. And much more aware of her own body than was usual, which, given the company she was in, could be regarded as distinctly dangerous. 'They're okay, I suppose,' she said ungraciously. 'Or at least they'll do for the time being.'

But Kadir didn't react to her clumsy rejection of his offerings, he just slanted her another devastatingly cool smile. 'Look, why don't we take a walk around the palace gardens before dinner?' he suggested. 'The grounds are very beautiful when they're floodlit and a little fresh air might make you feel better.'

'I'll tell you what would make me feel better— getting someone to drive me back to the airfield so that I can jump on a plane and not have to keep looking at your smug face!'

'Oh, Caitlin, Caitlin,' he murmured. 'Repetition is never an attractive quality. You really are going to have to find something different to talk about. No harm is going to befall you, Morag, or our child, of that I give you my word. And you wouldn't really want to fly back tonight, would you? Not when Cameron is tucked up so peacefully in bed.'

Caitlin's pulse accelerated. She wished he wouldn't *do* that either. Talk to her in that cool and measured way, as if she were an out-of-control hysteric and he were Mr Reasonable—when actually he was the one who was guilty of kidnap. An accusation she had flung at him on more than one occasion but which seemed to keep washing over him. In fact, he hadn't actually responded to *any-thing* she'd said to him, so far. It was like trying to demolish a brick wall by hitting it with a feather.

Maddeningly, Kadir had been nothing but diplomatic from the moment their motorcade had arrived at his impressive palace, whose soaring towers, golden cupolas and domed windows had taken her breath away yet also managed to daunt her with its sheer size and majesty. Not wishing to distress Cameron, she had forced herself to behave with exaggerated politeness towards the man who had brought them here without permission—and her own acting ability had taken her by surprise. Why, to the casual observer, she and the Sheikh might have seemed like a pair of amicable partners as he led her through the seemingly endless marble corridors and pointed out the many attractions of the royal palace along the way, sounding once again a bit like the seasoned tour guide he had seemed back in London.

'This is the recreational library, and in here are volumes in English of just about every classic book ever written, but my staff will always be able to get their hands on anything you can't find.'

'Thank you,' she had replied stiffly, though her eyes had widened with anticipation on seeing rows and rows of beautifully bound books in a stunning room which overlooked a dramatic sculpture garden.

'And here is the film room.' He had opened the door so that Caitlin could peer in at a luxurious space with twenty comfortable seats and a screen as large as her local cinema at home. 'I have arranged for many suitable children's movies to be available for Cameron, that's if you are happy for him to watch them.'

'Thank you,' she had repeated, because it had seemed churlish to do otherwise. But that thin veneer of civility she was presenting to the outside world didn't hint at the bitter truth which was raging inside her like a boiling cauldron.

That she felt as if she had walked into a living nightmare...forced into unwilling proximity with a man she resented and desired in equal measure.

Yet, Cameron had shown no such reserve, happily greeting whoever passed him and generally behaving as if to the manor born. As if he were used to being surrounded by a gaggle of doting servants. As if, on some fundamental level, he understood that one day all this would be his. How could she, his mother, have then created a scene—grabbing at the arm of the first senior official they met and demanding to be allowed to call the British Ambassador before being ferried home?

To Caitlin's fury, Kadir had also been right about Morag, who hadn't reacted to being spirited off to a far-off desert country with any of the indignation Caitlin might have expected from the middle-aged matron. In fact, she had actually smiled and remarked that nothing like this had ever happened to her before and she was quite enjoying the adventure—not to mention the prospect of spending an unspecified amount of time in a royal palace, especially one which had such beautiful gardens.

'But we're being kidnapped!' Caitlin had snapped as they had been shown into the large part of the palace which had been given over to them and whose north-western light Kadir had insisted was the best.

'Well, you keep saying that and I suppose that is one way of looking at it, dear. But Cameron doesn't seem to mind and neither do I. And the boy really *should* get to know his father, Caitlin, especially since he's a king.' Morag had given a sigh which had sounded positively girlish. 'And a desert king, at that. Why, it's like something out of a fairy story!'

Caitlin remembered blinking at her in astonishment. Whoever would have put the normally staid nanny down as a romantic?

But Morag had recently retired to her own suite of rooms which adjoined Cameron's—citing jet lag as her excuse to miss dinner and have an early night and leaving Caitlin alone with Kadir in a way which felt almost premeditated. As if he were planning to target her when she was on her own and at her most vulnerable.

Was he?

Because if that was the case she must not let him.

They needed to talk, yes. They needed to discuss 'the situation', as he had described it so infuriatingly on the plane. What they didn't need—or rather what *she* didn't need—was to wander around the dreamy-looking palace grounds, all washed in moonlight, which had painted the statues a glowing silver. Because wasn't the faux romance of her surroundings making her have thoughts which were very troubling? Thoughts which involved Kadir taking her into his arms and kissing her again— except that this time she wasn't certain she'd be able to stop it from going any further. She let out a heavy sigh. Her body felt so *responsive* when he was close—as if it had been programmed to react that way around him, and all the reasoning in the world didn't seem to make the slightest difference. And wasn't her physical vulnerability a warning sign that she needed to be on her guard against her own feelings, for fear of where they might take her?

Which was why she shook her head in answer to his suggestion—no matter how much the potent perfume of the frangipani cried out to her to inhale it long and deeply. Because she needed to be strong. She must never forget that she was on *his* territory, and he was a king. An all-powerful king with hot and cold running servants and what seemed like no contact with the outside world. And she was going to have something to say about *that*.

'No, thanks,' she said, as she heard a nearby clock beginning to toll the first of eight chimes. 'I'd rather just go straight into dinner. For this discussion about our future which we're supposed to be having.'

He inclined his robed head, his black eyes glittering and unreadable. 'As you wish. Please. Follow me.'

Kadir kept his eyes straight ahead as Caitlin accompanied him, though it was difficult not to be diverted by her athletic grace, which made the filmy material of her robe cling rather distractingly to her bottom as she walked. Stepping back, he ushered her into one of the less intimidating dining rooms, where a table had been set with crystal and gold and festooned with crimson roses. He watched as she glanced around the room, as if committing it all to memory, and once again he found himself mesmerised by the red-gold gleam of her hair, which was highlighted by the fractured gleam from the chandeliers.

He felt his pulse quicken. In truth, he could hardly believe she was here—or that his audacious plot had proved quite so effective. Such dramatic and high-blown behaviour wasn't his usual modus operandi—and he was aware that by behaving in such a way, he was helping perpetuate the common myth of desert kings being nothing but primitive men who simply stormed in and took what they wanted. Yet Kadir had seen his actions as his only option and in a crazy kind of way it had felt *right*. For hadn't he secretly enjoyed playing the powerful macho sheikh and showing the pale Scottish redhead exactly who was boss? And hadn't she brought such a drastic measure on herself? If she hadn't been so intransigent in her dealings with him, they could have worked out a far more conventional way for her to arrive in his homeland, with young Cameron in tow.

But in reality he couldn't really envisage any other solution than this. Even if she had been amenable to future visits, would he have readily waved goodbye to his son—even temporarily—and left him behind? How did he know he could trust her—and that she wouldn't try to keep his son away from him again, as she had already done for four long years?

Once again he felt a flicker of regret as he thought about how much of Cameron's young life he had missed. But coupled with that regret was a complex cocktail of feelings which did not sit comfortably with him, for he could not deny his own part in what had happened. Just as he could not deny that his desire for Caitlin was as intense as ever. It still pulsed through his body each time he saw her, despite the fact that she made no effort to adorn herself.

And she never had done, he reminded himself grimly. If she had, he might have been on his guard when he'd stumbled across her on that wild Scottish moor.

Memories came back to taunt him. The first time she had touched his naked body, he had felt as if he might dissolve. And when he had joined with her... He swallowed. When he had spread wide her glistening folds to thrust deep inside her warm and liquid heat, he hadn't known where he ended and she began. Many times he had wondered if that was the effect she had on all men.

Yet he didn't want to feel like this. As if he could explode with frustration every time she came close—a visceral need to be inside her again.

So what was the secret of her enduring appeal? he wondered. Was it the flame of her hair, which contrasted so vividly with that pale, freckled skin? Or eyes which were the colour of a Xulhabi spring sky—the most delicate blue you could imagine? Clear, soft eyes, fringed with pale lashes. When he'd met her, she had been ignorant of his status—something which had made her unusually candid in his company—and that had been rare enough for him to be charmed by her.

Was it that simple charm combined with a powerful sexual awakening which had stamped her memory so indelibly on his mind all these years? Which had haunted him during the long years of battle so that his promise to himself had been, *If I survive this, then I must see her again.*

It had proved a powerful enticement—powerful enough for him to ignore the wound which had gushed from his thigh and the fact that he had been forced to go without water for almost two days. He had nearly died during that last battle—that long and bloody battle, during which he had lost his one true friend and ally.

Rasim had been like a brother to him. Yet despite his strength and seeming indestructibility, he had lain broken and mortal as he'd breathed his last in the Sheikh's arms. Kadir remembered staring down at the waxen death mask of his friend in shock, and the reality of that awful image had almost taken him under. But a vision of Caitlin had sustained him as he'd hovered on the edge of consciousness—her pale face and bright hair never allowing him to slip into timeless oblivion. No wonder he hadn't been able to shift her from his mind afterwards, for he had associated her with his own personal resurrection.

He made no further comment until they were seated on opposite sides of the table and he observed her glancing somewhat askance at the gleaming array of solid golden knives. 'Just work from the outside in,' he advised, with a sudden flicker of benevolence.

'I *know* that,' she replied, with force. 'I may live in the north of Scotland, but I have actually visited a restaurant before!'

He gave a sudden laugh and saw a startled servant turn and look at him, before quickly composing himself and busying himself with the drinks. And now Kadir found himself wondering how long it was since he had laughed out loud.

'Forgive me for my presumption,' he murmured.

'It's something I'm fast coming to associate with you.'

'It comes with the job—and the territory. People neither wish nor expect their leader to prevaricate. It makes them feel safer if he is prepared to go out on a limb to make the right decision,' he acknowledged drily.

'And do you?' she challenged. 'Always make the right decision?'

'Not always,' he said, in a surprisingly candid admission. 'But on balance, yes.'

'How unsurprising that your ego is so healthy, Kadir.'

Unapologetically, he shrugged and waited until the servant had filled their goblets and various dishes of local delicacies had been placed in front of them, then dismissed the hovering staff.

'So,' he began, once they had both picked at their

food without much interest. 'You are happy with your accommodation, I hope?'

She gave a little *tsk* at this and her fork clattered down onto her plate with a gesture of irritation she didn't bother to hide. 'I'm hardly going to complain about a suite of rooms the size of a football stadium, am I? Or the fact that whenever I so much as cough, a servant comes running to find out whether there's anything I need.'

He inclined his head. 'I will take that as an affirmation.'

'Kadir,' she said, giving an impatient sigh as she took a sip of water. 'We can't sit here pretending that nothing's happened. I want us to go home. All of us,' she added pointedly.

He spread his hands out, the palms opening towards her in an expansive gesture. 'In theory, nothing is preventing you from leaving.'

'In theory, yes. But you are perfectly aware that I don't have the means to get myself to the airport. And although most of your servants speak English, every time I ask someone if they can arrange to have a car sent for us in the morning, they act mystified.' She drew a deep breath. 'Although I notice they understand perfectly well when I request another jug of water or for Cameron to have a slightly firmer pillow!'

'Caitlin—'

'And another thing,' she continued, barely giving herself time to draw breath. 'Every time I've tried to use my phone, it's failed to connect. And the Internet isn't working either.' She glared at him. 'Almost as if there was some malevolent blocking device at work!'

'Nothing malevolent about it, I can assure you,' he returned smoothly. 'The signal is notoriously bad here. We're in the middle of the desert, for heaven's sake!'

'My point exactly. So will you please get us out of here?' she said, from between clenched teeth. 'ASAP.'

Kadir carefully set down his goblet and leaned back to study her. 'You know I can't do that, Caitlin.'

'Can't, or won't?'

Unwillingly Kadir felt another smile tug at his lips, because her feistiness was exhilarating. Uncomfortably so. He could feel the heavy pulse of his blood and his groin had grown so hard that it was impossible to think straight. Difficult to concentrate on anything other than how much he hungered to see the splendour of her naked body again and to feel her in his arms. But he forced himself to put such distracting thoughts aside, because lust would weaken him. Would detract him from his primary purpose.

'All I'm asking for is time for Cameron to get to know me. I would like to do those things I promised him. To show him the palace stables and take him to the capital of Azraq so that he can see the mighty golden dome for himself. To teach him chess and educate him about his ancestors. There is a whole rich culture here of which he is ignorant. Is it not fair for the child to realise that he is part Xulhabian as well as part Scottish?'

She seemed to give this some consideration. In fact, she picked up a glistening slice of iced white peach and chewed on it thoughtfully, before speaking. It was her first obvious enjoyment of her food she had been given, he noted, and he was surprised at how good that made him feel.

'And after that you'll let us go?' she said.

His benevolence vanished and Kadir sighed, because either she wasn't getting the point or she was refusing to see it. Or perhaps he had been a little too vague. Surely she must have realised that he wasn't just going to let them go. To do what? For Caitlin to return to her old life and perhaps seek out a man willing to marry her and for their son to be brought up as an ordinary islander? His mouth twisted. Did she really imagine he would allow his only child to think of another man as a father figure?

Perhaps he needed to demonstrate to her that there could be no other father for Cameron.

And no other man for her.

He lifted a damask napkin to his lips. 'If that's what you want, then of course I will allow you to leave. All I'm asking is that you allow a little time for you and Cameron to get to know Xulhabi better.'

'How much time?' she demanded.

He studied her with calculating eyes. 'Shall we say a few weeks?'

'A few *weeks*?'

'That seems reasonable.'

'To you, maybe.'

'So you're agreed?' he said, his air of finality bringing to an end her objections.

She shunted out a breath, but the faint nod of her head indicated that she had finally seen sense. 'I suppose so.'

'Good.' He was careful to keep any sense of triumph from his voice. 'And now, let's talk about something else. We've spoken about so many things—'

'You can say that again,' she said darkly, and he might have smiled, if he weren't determined to discourage interruption.

'But one thing is still glaringly absent,' he continued smoothly.

She leaned forward, reaching towards a silver dish of salted almonds. 'Oh? And what's that?'

'So far all the information seems to have been coming from my direction. Isn't it also time you told me something about your past, Caitlin Fraser?'

CHAPTER SEVEN

CAITLIN, HER HAND hovering over a bowl of almonds, stilled. 'My past?' she echoed.

'That's right,' he agreed.

'And…' she licked her dry lips, laying the blame on the salty almonds '…what do you want to know exactly?'

'It's not too difficult. The usual things. Where you were born and how you spent your childhood.' Kadir shrugged. 'It has occurred to me that I know practically nothing about the mother of my child.'

She pushed the nuts away and glared at him. 'Didn't your spies find out for you when they were tracking me down?'

'My emissary came back with very little concrete information,' he admitted. 'He discovered you were living on a small Scottish island and had borne a son who bore an uncanny resemblance to me, and that your mother had died many years before. Other than that, nothing. There was no mention of a father on your birth certificate.'

'You looked at my *birth certificate*?'

'Why wouldn't I?' he questioned coolly. 'In the same situation, wouldn't you have endeavoured to gather as much information as possible?'

Caitlin returned the burn of his black gaze, her heart pounding hard beneath her thin tunic. She felt fear and she felt dread, which easily eclipsed her outrage that he had gone poking around in her past. Because everyone had a secret they would prefer the world not to know, and he was about to discover hers.

If she chose to tell him.

She had never talked about it with anyone, mainly because she'd never got close enough to someone to want to confide in them. Or for the layers of her painful past to be peeled away, leaving her exposed and vulnerable. Except for this man, of course. She'd been closer to Kadir than to anyone, but it had only been a very fleeting intimacy and it had only ever been physical. It made her feel a little foolish now to realise just how spiky and unrounded she must be as a human being, that she should have considered the twelve hours she spent with Kadir as the most significant twelve hours of her life. How sad was that?

But those hours had produced a beautiful child. His child. And didn't that make his question not only understandable, but reasonable? Didn't he have the right to know something about her, as she did him? And he had already obliged by confiding in her the bitter truth about his marriage.

Nonetheless, it wasn't easy to address a subject she'd spent much of her life trying to forget, and a moment or two passed before Caitlin was ready to speak. And wasn't it funny how something could still hurt, even after all these years? It was like poking at a scar you thought had completely healed, only for it to surprise you by starting to bleed again.

'There was no mention of my father on the birth certificate because my mother didn't name him,' she began.

His eyes became shuttered so that all she could see was the ebony gleam which shone from between the thick lashes. 'Why not?'

She paused. *Say* it, she told herself. Just say it. It's not a big deal in this modern world, not like in the old days. But it still felt like a big deal to her. 'Because he already had a wife and other children and he begged her not to. In fact, he did his best to try to persuade her not to give birth to me in the first place. But fortunately, she chose to ignore his advice and incentives.' She gave a bitter laugh. 'It was the one sensible thing she did throughout the whole of my childhood.'

'Caitlin.'

The shock on his face was almost palpable as he said her name but Caitlin couldn't resist a dig, even though the comment probably hurt her far more than it could ever hurt him. 'Perhaps now you'll understand my shock when I discovered you were married.'

'I am only just beginning to realise the impact that discovery must have had on you,' he said gravely, before giving a heavy sigh. 'So your mother had a brief affair with a married man?'

Just like you.

He didn't actually come out and say that, but the words hung in the air just as clearly as if he had. Caitlin could feel her cheeks begin to burn, knowing that she didn't have to justify herself because this wasn't about her—they were supposed to be talking about her mother. But she went ahead and did it anyway.

'It was nothing like what happened with us. Because she *knew* he was married. At least she was given the choice about whether or not she wanted to get involved,' she retorted, and saw him flinch—but strangely, his obvious discomfiture gave her no pleasure. 'She used to work for him, until she got pregnant, and then she left, supposedly by mutual agreement, though basically she was told to go or she would get fired. But the affair continued for years, based on a promise my father made that he would divorce his wife and marry my mother. Which he never did, of course.'

Kadir's eyes narrowed. 'And did you ever meet him?'

'Only once, but I was too young to remember much about it, or maybe I just blocked it out. Apparently, he wasn't exactly thrilled to have a child who had been born out of wedlock—a child with the potential to upset his pampered life as a city boss. And then it all turned sour. My mother started to get needy. She…' Caitlin swallowed, because this bit she *did* remember. She wished she could have forgotten it, but the mind could prove remarkably stubborn when it came to selective memory. 'She started to make demands. Started setting ultimatums, which were never met, so she'd set another one, and then another. Then she threatened to ring his wife and tell her about me…'

'What happened?' he questioned, as her words tailed off.

'He met up with her one day and told her he had already confessed to his wife.' She vividly remembered the use of the word confession. A word associated with sin. Had that association contributed to Caitlin's failure to interact successfully with the opposite sex, once she'd come of age? She didn't know and right now it wasn't particularly relevant. All she knew was that Kadir was still looking at her with curiosity burning from those ebony eyes—and she was going to finish her story. She had to—because what good would it do if they continued to be strangers to one another? 'He told her he never wanted to see her again, nor me.'

Now why had her voice started wavering? Why did she care about the rejection of a man who had never wanted her born? She cleared her throat, drank some pomegranate juice and continued. 'And he didn't. See me, that is. We were living on Cronarty by then. My mother never really recovered from his rejection. She kind of went to pieces—and when we heard that he'd died very suddenly she insisted we go to the funeral to pay our respects.' Caitlin shivered, wishing she'd brought one of her thick Scottish sweaters down to dinner with her after all.

Her mother had been slightly drunk and very determined—and no words of Caitlin's had been able to make her see sense. At eight years old she'd been powerless to prevent her mother from taking her along to the service, where she had made the discovery that her birth father had been a very rich and powerful man indeed. She remembered the sickly scent of the white lilies which had been massed outside the huge church and the startled faces of the black-clothed mourners when they had appeared. Sobbing, her head dramatically covered with an ebony mantilla, her mother had dragged Caitlin towards the door but someone must have worked out who they were.

'And?' Kadir prompted.

Caitlin bit her lip. It had been the single most embarrassing event of her life. 'We weren't wanted there—obviously. Two women stepped forward. They were the most beautiful women I'd ever seen.

They must have been a decade or so older than me. Their faces were icy and their eyes were filled with contempt. I remember they barely opened their lips as they spoke. They told us that if we didn't leave immediately of our own accord, then they would call security. I discovered afterwards that they were his daughters, too. But legitimate, of course.'

'By the desert storm!' To her surprise, Kadir had brought his fist crashing down hard on the table so that all the golden cutlery rattled. 'Why didn't you tell me this before?'

'When was I going to do that, Kadir?' she demanded. 'We didn't exactly do much talking at our first meeting, did we? Even if we'd had time, it's not really the best conversational ice-breaker in the world. And when you found me again, you were too busy being angry and taking control of all our lives for me to want to bring it up. Anyway, what difference does it make?'

Kadir shook his head and for a moment he stared straight ahead in silence, as the tall candles guttered on the table between them. He couldn't put it into words, but it *had* made a difference. He felt the unexpected clench of his heart as he imagined her pain and humiliation at being ejected from the church. He could picture only too well the inebriated mother who had dragged her there. If he had been in full possession of those facts about her past, would he still have brought her out here, without her permission? He felt a stab of guilt. He didn't know. He could never know. But surely he could show her a little consideration from here on in.

'It is late and your eyelids are growing heavy,' he said softly, rising to his feet. 'I think we've said everything there is to be said for tonight. Come, Caitlin, I shall accompany you to your suite.'

'Thank you.' For a moment she looked a little taken aback by his kindness and then, in a flurry of ice blue silk, she got to her feet.

They walked towards her suite mostly in silence, though occasionally he took the time to point out a particularly beautiful artefact and, once, to pause at the circular window which, at least twelve times a year, framed the full moon. She made all the appropriate responses to his remarks but he thought she seemed preoccupied. And when they finally reached her door, Kadir could see uncertainty clouding her freckled face, which somehow pierced his conscience far more than her defiance had done earlier.

'Can I ask you something?' she said.

Unexpectedly, the corners of his lips twitched. 'You haven't held back so far.'

'Even though nothing I say ever achieves what I want it to achieve?' she returned, before sucking in a deep breath. 'But this is different.'

'Oh?'

She twisted her ringless fingers together before

looking him straight in the eye. 'It's important for us to monitor how well Cameron settles in, because I'm sure that even you…'

Her words tailed off and when she looked at him, there was something beseeching in her gaze.

'Even I, what, Caitlin?' he prompted sardonically.

'If we discover he's desperately unhappy and homesick. If, for example, he misses Hamish—'

'Hamish?' A sudden spear of jealousy shot through him. 'Who the hell is Hamish?'

'His hamster. Mrs McTavish is looking after him at the moment. They have another two hamsters so it's no bother for her.' She hesitated. 'But if, for any reason, he really wants to go home after a few days, then you'll let him?'

Kadir knew what she was doing and thought how clever she was. For he could hardly lay claim to wanting to be a good father if he then did the very thing which would make his child unhappy, could he? Slowly, he nodded, picking his next words with care. 'How can I refuse such a request?' he questioned. 'All I ask in return, is that you will do nothing to try to influence the child in his decision.'

Their eyes met in a long moment. 'Touché!' she said softly, and then she smiled.

It was a rueful smile but it was the first one he'd seen since re-entering her life and the effect of her soft curving lips momentarily captivated him. Her ice blue gaze pulled him in like a magnet and suddenly Kadir found he couldn't look away. And neither, it seemed, could she, for she was staring at him as if she were in a trance.

Clad in the traditional tunic of a high-born Xulhabian woman, she looked both strange and yet deeply familiar. Her long red hair tumbled all the way down her back and Kadir longed to feel those glossy tendrils trickling through his fingers once more.

He sensed that if he kissed her now he would meet no opposition. And he wanted that. He wanted that very badly. But with desire came the certain knowledge that Caitlin Fraser had once possessed the power to make him lose control, and he couldn't risk that happening again. Not right now. Not until he had achieved what he'd set out to achieve.

And that was the bottom line. This was all about Cameron and Xulhabi, not him. His own foolish and transitory desires must be sublimated for the time being. He must determine his son's claim on the land he would one day inherit and nothing could be allowed to divert him from that aim.

Because while desire ebbed and flowed like the tide, he must be nothing but steadfast when it came to the continuity of his bloodline.

CHAPTER EIGHT

CAITLIN COULDN'T SLEEP.

Despite lying between linen sheets as fine as gossamer on a spacious bed which could have slept a family of four, she was disturbed by images of Kadir's searing black gaze as he had bade her goodnight after dinner last night. She couldn't believe that she had confided in him so honestly and told him more than she'd ever confessed to another living soul, considering it to be nobody's business but her own. Even Morag knew only the very barest facts about her background.

But Kadir had lulled her into a frank disclosure about her mother and father, before walking her to her suite of rooms and then leaving her in a swirl of kingly finery. The atmosphere around them had felt loaded with tension and for a moment she'd thought he was going to kiss her again. And, when that had failed to materialise—hadn't she convinced herself she was relieved? That had been total self-delusion, of course—because she would have liked nothing more than to have been cradled within the warm power of Kadir's embrace.

After checking on a sleeping Cameron, she had gone to bed but the night provided no immunity against forbidden thoughts, and suddenly she found herself wide awake and at the mercy of her senses. She kept remembering how it had felt to have Kadir's hands and lips on her body—brushing with devastating accuracy over her belly and breasts. At one point she awoke, her nipples aching and her skin bathed in sweat, aware of an aching deep inside her which wouldn't seem to go away. In the end she gave up chasing that elusive slumber, shutting herself in the bathroom while it was still dark outside, and standing beneath the power shower as she blitzed her body and her hair. By the time dawn was glimmering on the horizon, she was already dressed and raring to go.

Her nerves felt jangled as she waited for Cameron to wake up, forcing herself to lie back against the pillows on the huge bed and watch as the garden was gradually lit by soft shades of rose and gold. She had given Kadir her word she wouldn't attempt to influence their son in any way, but she couldn't believe her little boy would want to stay in this remote place, so far from everything he knew. She couldn't *let* herself believe it—because that offered a glimpse of a future which terrified her. A future in which her own position was uncertain. What place would she have in a culture like this?

Would she become the faceless Englishwoman unwillingly tolerated because she was the mother of the future King? She swallowed. She would give it a few days, as promised, and then quietly ask Cameron what he wanted to do. And when, as expected, he complained of being homesick, she would convey his sentiments to Kadir.

The ticking of the Ottoman clock was hypnotic and she must have dozed off, because when her eyes snapped open it was fully light and she could hear the distant bustle of life in the corridors of the palace. Hastily, Caitlin barged into the adjoining suite of rooms to find Cameron's bed…

She blinked in dismay.

Empty.

Morag was in the next room and at first Caitlin didn't recognise her because her ample frame was clothed in a flowing robe instead of her usual elasticated trousers and comfy top. She was sitting alongside a veiled female servant as the two of them companionably folded unfamiliar garments into a neat pile. They looked up in slight alarm as Caitlin came bursting in through the door.

'Where's Cameron?' she demanded.

Morag smiled. 'Ach, he was awake ages ago! Running around as excited as I've ever seen him. The Sheikh has taken him down to the stables.'

'Has he had breakfast?'

'The Sheikh said they would eat upon their return.'

'Oh, did he?' questioned Caitlin, trying to keep her voice light. 'You should have woken me.'

'The Sheikh said that you must be tired after your long journey and we should let you sleep.'

'I'll bet he did.'

She wanted to ask Morag if she realised that she sounded like a tame parrot with 'the Sheikh' this and 'the Sheikh' that, but Caitlin realised that would be taking her temper out on the wrong person. And besides, she needed Morag on her side. Turning to the servant who was seated alongside her, she tried to summon the semblance of a smile. 'Do you think you could show me the way to the stables?'

'Certainly, mistress. I will go and find Makim and ask him.'

She returned minutes later with Kadir's aide by her side and he chatted equably as he led Caitlin from the suite, even though his attempts at conversation were met only with politely monosyllabic responses because she didn't trust herself to say what was really on her mind. At least—not to him.

But she was unprepared for her emotional reaction when eventually they tracked Cameron down to the state-of-the-art stables on the eastern side of the palace and Caitlin felt as if she were looking at the scene through the wrong end of a telescope, because it was so…unexpected. And never before had she felt quite so redundant as a mother. Or so excluded.

Her son was being held by his father and his little arms were locked tightly around his father's neck as Kadir crooned softly to the most beautiful horse Caitlin had ever seen, its glossy dark coat gleaming like a polished nut. It made such a perfect tableau that she almost wished she had her camera with her so that she could have captured the image, but her hands were trembling so much she doubted she'd have been able to hold the camera. Because all she could think was, *why had the Sheikh spirited away her son without telling her?*

Despite the heat she felt cold. An outsider. Someone who had no right to be there. A dark and nebulous fear began to creep over her as she took a step forward.

Did they hear her enter? Was that why Kadir suddenly turned and saw her, a brief flare of something she didn't recognise in his black eyes. Was it *resolve*?

'Caitlin,' he said softly.

She hated how her skin shimmered in response to the way he said her name as he bent to put Cameron down so he could come running over to her, black hair flopping into his eyes.

'Mummy! Mummy! Daddy's going to get me a pony so I can learn to ride! He says we can go and choose one!'

He looked up at her expectantly and Caitlin's heart sank as she bent to kiss his soft little cheek.

What could she say? *You won't be needing a horse, darling, because hopefully you won't be here long enough to ride it.*

But even she acknowledged that as a mean and selfish thought. Just as she acknowledged that if she reacted in any way other than positive, it would be like announcing to a class of excited youngsters that there was no such thing as Father Christmas.

'That's lovely, darling. I hope you said thank you,' she replied gamely.

'Indeed he did,' purred Kadir. 'The child's manners are faultless.'

And even though inside Caitlin was glowing with maternal pride at the compliment, she couldn't shake off her resentment towards the man who was making it. She felt manipulated and she wasn't quite sure how to liberate herself from that feeling. 'Good to know,' she said tightly, before turning to her son. 'Shall we go and have some breakfast now?'

Breakfast was obviously a poor substitute for being amongst a stable full of snorting thoroughbreds but Cameron nodded and obediently took his mother's outstretched hand.

She met Kadir's eyes, hoping that her gaze managed to convey the fact that she was seriously cheesed off. And confused. And out of her depth, like a novice swimmer who had stupidly jumped into the deep end of the pool. 'Please excuse us.'

'Of course.' He inclined his head. 'Makim will

show you the way back. I have some work I must attend to, if you don't mind?'

'I don't mind at all,' she said truthfully.

Because Kadir's company was the last thing she felt like right now. At least with Makim she wasn't plagued by doubts and feelings she wished would go away. Stupid, conflicting feelings which made her stupidly susceptible to the Sheikh's potent charisma, even though she resented his high-handed and deeply patrician attitude.

With Cameron chattering beside her, they returned to their expansive quarters and, once seated at the dining table, Caitlin forced herself to try and eat some breakfast. But she felt disorientated as she peeled an orange for her son and fanned the segments onto a plate. It occurred to her that she was still in a sense of shock. Everything had happened so quickly. Everything still *was* happening so quickly and she was just sitting back like a spectator and letting it. Maybe it was time she stopped being so passive around the mighty Sheikh, and started being a little proactive.

She and Cameron spent much of the morning in the swimming pool and, after lunch, Caitlin took her son on an extensive tour of the palace and the grounds. They played ping-pong in the games room, watched a cartoon about the travails of a mermaid with very similar hair colour to her own, and were just about to sit down to an early dinner with Morag when Kadir surprised them by making a sudden, unannounced appearance—heralded by an over-the-top display of deep bowing from the attendant servants. Annoyingly, Caitlin's heart started beating out a primitive tattoo of excitement as his dark figure dominated the entrance to the lavish dining room.

'Do you mind if I join you?' he questioned.

What could Caitlin say, when any words of objection would have been drowned out by Cameron's enthusiastic squeals and Morag's smiling agreement? 'Of course not,' she said coolly. 'Though you mustn't let us disrupt your routine if you prefer to eat dinner at eight?'

The brief flicker of his black eyes indicated he'd got her message loud and clear, but he continued walking towards the table, his robes flowing like rich cream over his hard body. 'Ah, but any disruption is not only necessary, but welcome. I realise I must be open to change if I am to carve out precious time with my son,' he replied smoothly, high-fiving Cameron as he slid into the seat beside him. 'And don't all the pundits say it's better to eat earlier, rather than later?'

Caitlin opened her mouth to reply, then shut it again. He had an answer for everything! She forced herself to eat some of the delicious food on offer and to listen as Kadir talked Cameron through some of the unfamiliar dishes on the menu. At other times he chatted affably to Morag, who started telling him about her love of historical fiction, which, to his credit, he managed to look enthusiastic about.

Meanwhile Caitlin sat there in frigid silence and all while Kadir's black eyes mocked her, as if daring her to say something. But she didn't want to make small talk. She wanted to talk to him about rules of behaviour concerning their son. About setting down guidelines he must agree to conform to while they were here. Basically, to assert her maternal rights and make him realise that he couldn't just push her into the shadows.

She was relieved by the time the meal ended and Morag began to gather up her young charge to get him ready for bed. She had just ushered him out of the room, when Caitlin turned to Kadir, who was also preparing to leave. 'Could I have a word with you, please?' she said, in a low voice.

He frowned. 'But you've had the opportunity to speak to me all evening, Caitlin, and you didn't say a word.'

'That was different. I didn't want to have this discussion in front of Cameron and Morag.'

'Why not?'

She shifted uncomfortably on her feet and flailed around for a coherent explanation which wouldn't seem as if she were only pursuing her own selfish interests. 'Because… Because…'

'Look.' Lifting his arm so that silk concertinaed

away from his wrist, he shot an impatient glance at his golden wristwatch. 'I have phone calls I need to make and I'm pretty tied up for the rest of the evening and most of tomorrow. Why don't we schedule in a time for Wednesday afternoon, when you might have worked out what it is you want to say to me? Come to my office. Shall we say three p.m.?'

She wanted to protest that now he was making her feel like a brainless fool, but instead Caitlin found herself nodding her agreement. Perhaps it made sense to address it that way. She would write down all her concerns in a list, just as she did when she took Cameron to the doctor. She would state her wishes calmly and clearly, so there could be no misunderstanding. And hopefully Kadir would be sensible enough to take note of them all. 'That sounds fine,' she said stiffly.

But she felt far from fine as she was led through the labyrinth of marble corridors at the appointed hour. Her nerves had been growing extremely frayed these past two days, and now her mouth was bone-dry with nerves—despite the fact that she'd gulped down a glass of iced water barely ten minutes ago. Was she really going to have the guts to lay down the law to a man like Kadir? Yes and yes and a million times yes. He might be *the* Sheikh, but he certainly wasn't *her* Sheikh.

The monarch's section of the palace was very different from her own quarters. It felt like a smooth and carefully oiled machine, with its quiet sense of purpose and people with files diligently going about their business. Passing through several outer offices, she was eventually shown into a lavish vaulted room, which was obviously the sole preserve of the King.

The room was empty and quickly she looked around, searching for clues about the man who inhabited it. A large desk dominated one side— a jewelled pot of golden pens contrasting rather comically with a computer and an array of phones. Over by some of the tall windows which overlooked the gardens was an informal area containing a luxurious divan, as well as a couple of ornate chairs. On a gleaming table stood a huge cut-glass bowl of orange roses, and on top of an inlaid bureau stood a small, framed photo of a man. And that was the only personal touch in a largely neutral room. No images of his mother were on show, she noted. Nor yet, any of Cameron.

Caitlin peered at the photo. Darkly handsome, the man wore traditional desert garb and looked about thirty. She wondered if it was an early photo of Kadir's father, but somehow it seemed too modern.

'Ah, you're here.'

The deep resonance of Kadir's voice interrupted her examination and Caitlin quickly straightened up, adjusting her tunic as she did so and wishing it were as easy to modify her racing heart. 'I am.'

SHARON KENDRICK 125

Kadir waited for her to ask about the photo he'd seen her looking at, but felt a huge wave of relief when she didn't, because right now he had no desire to delve into the past. Instead he concentrated on the slightly unbelievable fact that she was here, for no woman had ever been permitted entry into what was essentially his sanctum. As a space, it had always been sacrosanct—his and his alone, apart from the occasional necessary visit by his aides. But he had wanted to meet her away from the distraction of their son and his nanny, or the curious glances of the palace servants.

'So, Caitlin,' he said coolly. 'You wanted to speak to me?'

'Yes.' She cleared her throat. 'I think we need to clear a few things up.'

He raised his eyebrows. 'Please. Elaborate.'

'Well, obviously I can't stop you from just dropping in at mealtimes—'

'That's very generous of you,' he commented sardonically.

'But in future, I'd prefer if you didn't just take Cameron riding like you did on our first morning here, without having run it by me first.'

'Your objection being *what* exactly?'

'You should have woken me.'

'Should I? You'd had a long and emotional journey the previous day and had shown no sign of stirring. But Cameron wanted to make sure you were okay before we went off together, and so he looked in on you and told me you were still sleeping. On balance, I decided it was best not to disturb you.'

'Or maybe you just wanted to stake your claim on Cameron? To get him on his own so you could start influencing him.'

'Influencing him to do *what* exactly, Caitlin?'

She shrugged, biting her lip as if trying to hold back an unwanted tremble. 'Who knows? To turn him against me, perhaps. To push me out of the picture.'

He frowned. 'You really think I would do something like that?'

'How should I know what you'd do, Kadir? You put us on a plane and flew us halfway across the world—I wouldn't put anything past you! It was his first morning in a strange place. And in a palace, no less. He's never been anywhere like this before and it could have been very confusing for him.'

'But he seemed perfectly fine with it. And Morag agreed with my suggestion.'

'Of course she did. She would pretty much agree with anything you said because you've got her wrapped around your little finger!'

'The same certainly cannot be said of you,' he observed wryly. 'So tell me, Caitlin—what's *really* troubling you?'

She gave a frustrated wiggle of her hands. 'Surely you must realise that if you start promising him things—it's only going to create problems. Don't you think this kind of treatment is unbearably seductive for a small boy? Promises of ponies and palace pools. So that when he goes back to his other life—his *normal* life, on a tiny island in the middle of the Minch—it will be unbearably difficult for him to settle back in.'

Kadir met the fierce accusation of her gaze and an unexpected feeling of sadness washed over him as he listened to her heated accusations. Couldn't she see that everything was going to be different from now on? Was she really that naïve? 'But this *is* your new normal, Caitlin,' he said gently. 'Better get used to it.'

Some of the indignation left her eyes and was replaced by a flicker of apprehension. 'What are you talking about?'

He picked his words carefully. 'People already know you are here—that much was inevitable. My aides tell me that much comment has been made of Cameron's resemblance to me and that was inevitable, too. His identity cannot be kept a secret much longer. Sooner or later, the world is going to find out that he is my son and heir.'

'And doesn't he get any say in the matter?' she demanded. 'Don't I?'

He shook his head. 'This is not a question of who says what. He is my son. His destiny is written in the stars. Do you really think Cameron can just go back to his previous life and pretend nothing has changed? That he can carry on living on Cronarty?'

'But the island is as safe as houses,' she defended. 'The people there are very loyal. They won't make any kind of fuss, if I ask them not to.'

'Oh, Caitlin.' He shook his head. 'Now you really *are* being naïve. We aren't talking about an ordinary child. We are talking about the welfare of a future king and there are security issues at stake here. Big ones. My country is now at peace, but for many years we have been fighting a perilous war—and wars always create enemies. Don't you think Cameron will be vulnerable to threats from outside sources once his identity is known? Isn't that something you ought to consider before you take him back to a place where he will be largely defenceless against malevolent forces?'

He could see her lips folding in on themselves, as if she was trying very hard not to cry and that was not his intention. He didn't want to make her cry—and not just because he wasn't sure he was equipped to cope with a woman's tears. 'Caitlin—' He held out a hand towards her but she shook it away.

'I never meant for this to happen—to give birth to a future king!' she burst out. 'But you didn't give me the choice, did you, Kadir? You didn't tell me about all this royal stuff, because if you had, I could have turned around and run in the opposite direction!'

He stared at her, and as he saw the pain in her eyes something dark and unknown nagged away at… He furrowed his brow. Not his conscience, no. Something else. Something buried away deep inside him, but an instinctive measure of self-protectiveness made him quickly push the thought away. 'Yes, I should have told you,' he agreed huskily. 'But I couldn't. It wasn't even a deliberate decision—it just happened that way. And even if I *had* told you, do you really think you would have walked, Caitlin? Don't you think I tried myself and couldn't manage it?'

She shook her head so that fiery strands of hair flew around her narrow shoulders. 'That's…irrelevant.'

'No, it's not. Not then and certainly not now. It's still there, this…*thing* between us, and it won't seem to go away.' He shook his head. 'Don't you think it's time we stopped fighting it, Caitlin?'

She stared at him. 'You're talking about…desire?'

'Of course I am. What else could it be?' he husked. 'You must know how much I want you. And you want me, too. I can see it in your eyes and in your body. Why else do you shiver whenever I come near? And don't you think I shiver, too? Well, don't you?'

Caitlin swallowed as his black eyes glittered, his words firing up everything she already felt for him and igniting the smoulder of feelings she'd been trying to keep at bay. But this wasn't a fairy tale, she reminded herself bitterly. Nobody could accuse Kadir of building her up with false hopes. He wasn't professing love, or emotion. He was spelling out exactly what he felt for her, which was lust— no more and no less. It shouldn't have been enough and yet somehow...

She closed her eyes. Would it be so wrong to be intimate with the man who had fathered her child? Wasn't she allowed to enjoy her body, like other people? Last time around she'd been vulnerable. She'd started to believe she was falling in love with him but this time that wasn't going to happen. Why would it when Kadir had expressly told her that love was a trap?

But sex. Sex she could do.

'So what do you propose we do about it?' she asked him, her voice coming out all breathy.

He stilled, as if her easy assent had taken him by surprise, but quickly he reasserted his mastery. 'I'll tell you exactly what we're going to do. First we're going to get rid of the view.' He walked across to the wall and the touch of a button made electric blinds float silently down over every window, dimming the light so that it looked like a gilded and exotic boudoir. 'And next I'm going to kiss you.'

He was walking towards her, his black eyes glittering, his steps slow and deliberate. He was giving her time to change her mind, Caitlin realised.

But somehow, making her wait was only increasing the hunger she felt for him, so that by the time he stood in front of her and pulled her into his arms, she was almost on fire with need.

And suddenly he was kissing her and she was kissing him back. Kissing him hard—as if trying to imprint her mouth indelibly on his. And he was saying things against her lips—soft, urgent words in a language she didn't recognise.

'Kadir,' she whispered as his fingers curled possessively over her silk-covered breast and the nipple immediately sprang to life.

'I want you,' he said deliberately. And he picked her up and carried her across the gilded room, towards the wide divan and the powerful scent of orange roses.

CHAPTER NINE

WITH A SWIFT economy of movement, Kadir peeled off Caitlin's tunic, revealing the modest bra and pants she'd bought in a discount store in Edinburgh. As his hungry gaze raked over her, she wondered if he was used to his women wearing bewitching scraps of silk and lace and how she could possibly measure up against them. But the hot flash of his eyes and the growl which erupted from his lips seemed to imply he didn't feel in the least bit short-changed by her appearance.

He unclipped her bra and bent to slide her panties all the way down her thighs, effortlessly lifting her up so that they fluttered from her ankles, before setting her down again. He kissed her hair as he reached down to touch her breast, a slow, circling thumb making the nipple grow hard again.

'I have wanted to see you naked like this for so long,' he husked.

Her cheeks grew hot, but Caitlin was determined to match his matter-of-factness. Because emotional danger beckoned if she read too much into what was simply a biological act. 'And you,' she whispered. 'I have longed to see you naked, too.'

'Then what are you waiting for, Caitlin? Why don't you take off my clothes?'

His uneven words were coated with need and Caitlin trembled beneath their rush of elemental power. She had never undressed a man before and she'd certainly never undressed a powerful king of the desert. But there had to be a first time for everything, surely? Her hands were unsteady as they moved towards the hem of his robe, mainly because she could feel the heat of his body beneath the silk and knew what delights awaited her. Pulling the garment over his head, her fingers tightened around its voluminous folds, her breath catching in her throat as she realised that, unlike her, he was completely naked beneath.

And it was impossible not to stare at him. To feast her eyes on the broad shoulders and honed chest and gleaming olive skin. The narrow hips and muscular thighs and long, hard legs. But most of all, she couldn't seem to tear her gaze away from the thick pole of his erection which sprang from between his thighs, pale against the dark forest of hair.

'Do you like what you see, Caitlin?' he questioned softly.

She lifted her gaze to his face. He's playing a game with me, she thought, and maybe he wanted her to play it, too. Was that what long-parted lovers were supposed to do when they met up again? But what if you didn't know the rules of the game—when your only experience of sex had been one short night which had ended so abruptly? 'It's okay,' she said coolly, the fabric slipping from her fingers to the floor.

'Just okay?'

His black eyes challenged her and suddenly Caitlin wondered why she was even *trying* to flirt with someone who was light years ahead of her in terms of sexual experience. 'M-more than okay,' she admitted truthfully, the words coming out in a rush. 'Your body is beautiful.'

Was it her shaky praise which provoked the sudden tension in his body? Which made his eyes narrow before he bent to capture her lips again, searing them with a kiss which felt as if he were branding her with fire? Caitlin didn't know and somehow it didn't seem important. She just kissed him back as if her life depended on it, because hadn't she dreamt of doing this so many times during the long nights she'd spent alone, and then woken up frustrated in the morning to realise it had all been a dream?

He lifted her up and laid her down on the divan, the smoky expectation in his eyes leaving her boneless with longing as he began to stroke her. And Caitlin closed her eyes, giving herself up to the sensation as he began to explore her skin. Because

last time it had all been so new and she'd been
so overcome with emotion that she hadn't really
had the chance to appreciate what was happening,
but she wasn't going to allow that to happen this
time. No way. Instead of having pointless fantasies
about having found 'the man of her dreams', she
was going to concentrate solely on the physical.
On the way he was stroking her inner thigh with
a thoroughness which quickly had her squirming
with frustration. On the way his tongue was lick-
ing its way luxuriously over each nipple, so that she
wriggled with pleasure. The way he groaned when
she smoothed her hand over the jut of his hips and
stroked his curving satin-skinned buttocks. The
way his blunt tip brushed tantalisingly against her
belly, and already she could feel a little bead of
moisture there.

'Kadir,' she whispered.

He reached out to slide out a drawer from beneath the rose-covered table, before producing a
small square of foil which glinted in the dim light.
As he smoothed on the protection with a slow and
provocative deliberation, she wondered if he just
happened to keep those condoms there, or whether
the whole scenario had been a set-up. Again, her
cheeks grew warm and this time Kadir must have
noticed, because his black eyes were curious.

'Are you blushing?' he murmured.

'Not at all. I think the air-conditioning must be failing. It's very hot in here.'

Unexpectedly, he laughed before pulling her into his arms and suddenly words were forgotten because his mouth was on hers and his hand was back between her thighs. *Where it belongs,* she thought fiercely. But then her fingertips encountered the rough ridge of a small jagged scar, which snaked across his lower abdomen, and inexplicably she felt a sharp pain shooting through her. Almost as if she were experiencing second hand the hurt he must have felt at the time. She opened her mouth to ask who had caused it, who had inflicted such a wound on him—but by then his finger was brushing against her quivering bud and her brain wasn't functioning at all.

Her body was hungry and her need was intense. Her throat dried as he straddled her and she parted her legs to accommodate him. And at last he was inside her. Easing slickly into her waiting heat and not seeming to notice the hard dig of her nails as she clung to him.

She gasped with each delicious thrust he made— her fingers sliding over his sweat-sheened skin as he took her higher and higher, until she didn't think she could bear it any more. And suddenly she was falling. Falling in slow motion through a splinter of stars, vaguely aware of Kadir's body tensing and hearing his guttural cry as he jerked inside her, before gradually growing still.

For a while they just lay there, Caitlin staring at one of the intricate lanterns which dangled from the ceiling as a great swell of emotion rose up inside her. And stupidly, she wanted to cry. To let out the tears which were building behind her eyelids, no matter how hard she tried to blink them away. Which wasn't supposed to happen. Sex was supposed to provide release and remind her what she'd been missing—not leave her racked with regret and a deep ache at the thought of what she could never have.

'Why are you crying?'

To her consternation, Kadir's question made her aware that a tear had dripped onto the velvet divan and she turned her face away from him. She wanted to deny the accusation but then he would rightly accuse her of lying, so instead she dashed an angry fist against her wet cheek. 'It doesn't matter.'

'Was it really so awful?' he persisted softly.

She gave a short laugh. 'Oh, come on. You must know it was anything but.'

'Then I am at a loss to understand.' He stroked his finger between her breasts. 'How do men usually respond when you react like this?'

She thought about glossing over the remark, rather than opening it up for debate. But his wife had lied to him, hadn't she? And there was no reason for her to do the same. 'They don't respond in any way at all,' she said quietly. 'Because there hasn't *been* any other lover than you. I was a virgin the night I slept with you, in case you hadn't noticed. In fact, I'd never been intimate with any man before you, Kadir—and I haven't been intimate with any man since.'

There was total silence. A pause so long that time felt suspended. And when he spoke his voice sounded heavy. As if each word had been carved from some dark and unforgiving rock. 'Me neither.'

Bewildered now, Caitlin turned to look at him, but his eyes were closed, his dark lashes fringed against his olive skin, his hair startlingly black against the green velvet divan. 'Run that past me again,' she whispered.

He opened his eyes and she found herself caught in the ebony gleam of his gaze.

'Your first experience,' he said flatly. 'Well, it was mine, too. Nobody before and nobody since.'

She shook her head. 'I don't think I've understood that properly.'

'You have.'

'You're saying…are you saying I'm the only woman you've ever had sex with?'

Another pause. 'That's exactly what I'm saying.'

She hated the way the possibility of that made her feel. As if she were somehow special. As if something had marked her out and made her seem different. But that was a crazy hope without any foundation—and even giving it houseroom was dangerous. And besides, it didn't make sense. None of it did.

'I don't understand,' she whispered. 'How is it even possible? I mean, you're so...'

'So?'

In the dim light, she could feel herself blush but she was still so caught up in the thrill of that moment that she said something she probably shouldn't have done. 'So amazing,' she whispered. 'So how on earth can you have been a virgin?'

Kadir looked down at her flushed pink face and wondered why he had told her, but deep down he knew why. He owed it to her to tell her the truth, even though it was not the kind of admission most men would be happy making. Yet from the outset he had been comfortable with his sexuality and his decision to channel it as he saw fit. With his ability to discard the expectations usually associated with a virile and highly desirable man. Yet, having told her part of the story, surely it would be impossible to leave the rest of the matter unexplained. Did he really want to masquerade as something he wasn't?

'I wanted to be the greatest king there ever was,' he began, and as he saw her lips purse together he shook his head. 'No, *not* for the sake of my ego, Caitlin, but for the sake of my people, who had suffered greatly by the time I came to the throne. My forebears had served Xulhabi well—my father less so. Under his watch, this country had been subject to constant invasion and land grabs and, economically, we were lagging behind many of the other desert states.'

'Why? Did he…did he take his eye off the ball or something?' She gave an embarrassed shrug. 'I'm sorry. I don't know how this kingship thing works.'

'In a way, that's exactly what he did,' he conceded. 'But the rot set in when he married.'

'Isn't that a little…harsh?'

'Harsh, but true.' He flickered her a look. 'You may recall me telling you he married my mother for love?'

'Which you don't believe exists?'

'Oh, I believe it exists, all right,' he said slowly, his voice growing hard. 'Just not for me. Maybe the example I was shown by my parents was enough to warp my opinion for ever.'

'Tell me about them,' she said quietly, brushing a handful of hair away from her cheek.

He stared up at the ceiling. 'She was the youngest of seven sisters—beautiful and completely spoiled, by all accounts—and although my father was warned it was an unsuitable match, he would not listen. Ironic, isn't it? That I chose so carefully when selecting a bride. I wanted more than anything not to repeat the mistake of my father, which is why I picked a supposedly *suitable* princess.' He gave a bitter laugh. 'And look how that turned out. Which just goes to prove that the majority of relationships are doomed from the start.'

'So what happened?' she said.

He shrugged. 'He was completely obsessed with her and, in a way, that seemed to diminish her respect for him. And the more she played him for a fool, the more it seemed to feed his desire for her. He found himself unwilling to commit to the very demanding role of monarch because that would take him away from the wife he was so infatuated with. But she...' He stopped for a moment, wondering if there was any need to tell her this and then he thought—why wouldn't he tell her when he had come this far, when he had already broken the rule of a lifetime by confiding such intensely personal matters? 'She took a series of lovers, which broke his heart. His loyal courtiers tried to protect him— the less scrupulous ones took advantage. And he went to pieces.'

'And what about you?' she questioned cautiously. 'It must have affected you, too.'

He shook his head, determined his expression would show no sign of the pain which had hit him so hard as a child and made him feel even more isolated. 'I tried to block out as much of the chaos as possible. And then, when I was nineteen, my father died, and my mother soon afterwards, and by the time I acceded to the throne, everything was in a mess.'

She looked as if she wanted to ask him a question and he guessed that maybe she was too shy to frame the words. 'You want to know what all this has to do with celibacy?'

'Well, yes.'

'History has always acknowledged the power which abstinence from sex confers upon a man,' he said. 'Wasn't the great knight Lancelot eventually ruined by his weakness for a woman's flesh? And don't great sportsmen deprive themselves of sex before a big game, in order to achieve the highest honours in their field?'

'I guess so,' she said uncertainly.

'I vowed that I would enter my marriage without impediment, so I could offer my bride not just my untouched body and my fidelity, but intense pleasure, too. That is why I studied erotic texts so extensively for so many years, for there are many ancient books which provide comprehensive guidance on the subject.'

There was silence for a moment while she seemed to absorb this.

'But what about your wife?' she questioned eventually. 'Surely she wanted you to consummate your marriage?'

'It never got that far. Or rather, the subject remained purely academic and there was no consummation.' His mouth twisted. 'For there is only one thing which makes addicts happy and that is their chemical of choice. Adiya simply wasn't interested in sex, not at any time during our short marriage.'

'But why…?' She looked as if she was trying to understand. 'I mean, there must have been a thousand more suitable women to choose from, so why me?'

This was, Kadir realised, what Americans sometimes called the sixty-four-thousand-dollar question. Could he put his response to Caitlin Fraser down to frustration and lust and being in the right place at the right time? Of course he could, because what other possible explanation could there be?

'Just before I met you, I'd spoken to one of Adiya's doctors, who had explained that she could live in that vegetative state for many years and it was highly unlikely she would ever recover.' He swallowed. 'And I accepted that, as my destiny.'

He had decided to embrace the life which fate had afforded him. He would be a celibate king. So he had buried his once fervent desire to sire a child and had used his energies to rescue his battered homeland, throwing himself into a series of demanding battles to reclaim the areas of his country which had been unlawfully occupied.

The war had been won but he had lost Rasim, his oldest friend, and for a while that had derailed him. And then, on a business trip to the UK, he had seen Caitlin Fraser standing on a hillside with her camera, her flame-red hair calling out to him, the soft crumple of her lips imploring him to kiss her when she turned round to reproach him for frightening the eagle away. It had been the most overwhelming temptation of his life, even though many women had propositioned him. He had resisted them—but he hadn't been able to resist her. Like some tame puppet he had asked her to meet him for dinner—made physically vulnerable by a woman in a tweed skirt and a scratchy sweater. Of *course* he hadn't known she was a virgin—he had no template with which to compare his night with her. Nor she him. Yet she had been, he recognised with a sudden unwanted rush of exultation.

She had been a virgin, too.

'And why *me*?' he said suddenly, turning the question on its head. 'There must have been men who had tried it on with you before.'

Now it was Caitlin's turn to hesitate, but she saw no reason to hide the truth from him. She wriggled up the divan a little.

'Because I had an inbuilt fear of men. My mother may have failed in many of the more accepted parental skills, but she was very good at teaching me that men were never to be trusted. That men would do you down if you gave them the chance. If you're told something enough times, then eventually you start to believe it. Oh, I went out with people from time to time, but nobody ever lit my fire.'

'And what was so different about me?'

He had been irresistible, that was what. With his towering stature and flashing black eyes, he had seemed more like someone who had stepped from the pages of a story. But what she'd felt for Kadir had transcended the physical. When she had talked to him it was as if she'd known him all her life, as if there were no barriers between them, nor ever could be. And when he had kissed her, she'd believed she could trust him with not just her body, but her heart and soul, too. The reality had been very different, of course. Maybe her mother had been right all along.

She wanted to hurt him as he had hurt her. To tell him she had fallen into bed with him because he had obviously been very rich and that had turned her on. But that wouldn't have been true and, anyway, he was the father of her child and they needed to find some way to work through this seemingly impossible situation in which they found themselves.

She reached down and touched her finger against the ridging scar which marred the perfection of his body. 'This is new,' she said quietly.

He nodded as he laid his palm over the faint stretch marks left behind after her pregnancy. 'So are these.'

It was unexpectedly poignant, this unspoken ac-
knowledgement of the time which had passed and
the ways in which they'd both changed. For a moment the atmosphere became undeniably intimate
and Caitlin was fearful of the way it made her feel.
'What happened?' she said, quickly moving the
conversation on.

For a moment he didn't reply and she half
thought he wasn't going to. But then he spoke and
she had never heard a voice sound quite so heavy,
or defeated.

'It was just at the end of the war with Yusawid
and the final push to reclaim our borders. I was
leading from the front but I was badly wounded,
and Rasim came to my assistance, and he...' His
voice sounded thick. 'He saved his king but lost his
own life in the process.'

'That's the man in the photo on your desk?'

He nodded. 'That's him. Rasim and I grew up
together. We learned to play and fight together and
he was more like a brother to me, despite the fact
that his mother was a palace servant. But he was
the only person who was ever there for me in an
atmosphere of poison and hate.' He turned to her.
'Can you understand now why the future of Xulhabi means so much to me, Caitlin? Can't you see
that if I fail to secure the continuation of the line, I
will also be failing the man who gave his life, not
for me, but for his country?'

Yes, she could understand all that. She bit her lip. But wasn't he asking too much of a child who was not yet five?

He had started stroking her breast again and wasn't it crazy how one minute you could literally be discussing life and death and in the next you could be opening your mouth so that your lover could put his tongue inside it? Maybe that was nature's way of protecting them from life's hardships—by making it possible for pleasure to eclipse the pain.

So many conflicting feelings were buzzing around her head and there were still questions she needed to ask. But not now. Not when Kadir's dark head was moving towards hers.

Because how could she possibly think about anything when he was kissing her like this?

CHAPTER TEN

INDOOR SWIMMING POOLS were pretty much the same the world over, Caitlin thought. Even a grand palace version of a pool didn't differ much from what you might find in a public bath. There was still all that echo and amplification of sound. Still the glimmer and shimmer of water beneath overhead lights which made everything seem supernaturally bright.

She stood in one of the recesses of the giant complex, shadowed and unobserved as she watched the deft movements of Cameron and Kadir playing together in the turquoise water.

Father and son.

From here it was achingly obvious that there could never be any question of Cameron's parentage.

Except that there was. At least, according to the dictates of ancient Xulhabian law it had to be proved.

She felt another twist of frustration as she recalled the conversation she'd had with Kadir, early last week. A conversation which had seemed doubly insulting in view of the fact that they had just had the most amazing sex.

Apparently, a tiny sample of her son's blood had been required.

'Blood?' Caitlin remembered echoing, rolling across the expanse of rumpled sheets and looking at him as if he were some kind of moonlighting vampire.

'It's no big deal. It is simply to ensure that there can never be any legal challenge.' His voice had been smooth but explicit. 'This will cover us in case there is ever any dispute about Cameron's right to rule. A kind of insurance policy, if you like.'

Caitlin had been so taken aback that she had found herself nodding her consent, without really thinking it through. Not thinking about all the implications which lay behind that supposedly simple remark. Why had she agreed so readily? For the sake of her son, or because she and Kadir seemed to have reached a plateau of understanding—almost of peace—and she wanted to maintain that situation for as long as possible? Had she maybe been seduced by the hope—no matter how hard she tried to deny it to herself—that the intimate moments they'd been sharing were something worth building on?

But she had flinched as a tiny needle was inserted into her son's perfect skin, and it was only afterwards that Kadir's statement had sunk in properly. He was still taking it as a given that Cameron would one day inherit his crown, when they still hadn't come to an agreement about that.

'Daddy! Daddy! Look!'

She watched Cameron dive beneath the dappled surface to swim an entire underwater width of the pool. And while he might have been bathing in Cronarty's lochs since he'd been little more than a toddler, he certainly hadn't been able to do *that* before they'd arrived here. She expelled an unsteady breath. Maybe it was true that plenty of money and resources were ultimately the most effective way of teaching a child something. She continued to watch as Kadir mimicked his son's movements, except that he managed an entire *length* of the pool, which made Cameron clap his hands together in delight. Was there *anything* the desert King wasn't good at? she found herself thinking.

Yes.

He wasn't very good at making her feel *connected* to him, for all that she shared his bed each night and revelled in the mind-blowing reality of his lovemaking. Because they weren't connected. Not really. Despite their semi-shared living situation, his bed and his body were all she had of him, for the confidences shared on their first night together had never been repeated.

And maybe *lovemaking* was too optimistic a way

of describing what took place every night in her bedroom, into which Kadir crept once darkness had fallen, before taking his leave as the sun was rising.

She was his secret.

Sometimes she thought she was his *guilty* secret.

'I am simply protecting your reputation,' was his reply to her studiedly casual question about her status. 'If it were openly acknowledged that you are my lover, it could create intrigue within the palace and that is always unwise. Let's leave it until we have come to a decision about where we go from here.'

And where was that? Caitlin had wanted to ask. But something held her back from asking the kind of questions which might provide difficult answers. Because while she couldn't imagine staying here, she couldn't imagine going back to Cronarty either. At least, not yet.

In an attempt to create some semblance of family life, she had joined in with the daily riding sessions which Cameron shared with his father. At first she had simply watched from the sidelines, but one morning Kadir had persuaded her onto a placid mare, even though it had been many years since she'd been in the saddle. His words had been soft and encouraging and she had found her gentle ride exhilarating—almost as exhilarating as the satisfaction in the Sheikh's eyes and Cameron's delighted whoops of excitement.

Sometimes, once the fierce heat had leached from the afternoon, Kadir would demonstrate the skills of Himyar, his prized falcon, while she and Cameron watched it circle and swoop before landing on the Sheikh's forearm, where it sat regarding the world with its clever, beady eyes. And he kept his promise to teach Cameron chess—a game which the boy was already beginning to understand and to love.

Yet sometimes Caitlin felt as if she were living in a parallel universe. To the outside world they were nothing but polite parents who were coexisting in relative harmony. Given Kadir's position of absolute power, nobody ever questioned them about their relationship. Nobody, other than the taciturn nocturnal guard, was aware that each night Kadir would slip into her darkened room and Caitlin would be on fire with unbearable desire as he took her in his arms. For two relative novices to sex, they certainly seemed intent on making up for lost time. And didn't it give her a buzz to think that Kadir had never done this with anyone else before—that each discovered pleasure was unique to them?

If only it were so simple to regulate her mood. To keep at bay the unwanted emotions which came flooding out of nowhere to tug at her heart. Sometimes she would find herself overcome with unrealistic yearnings—partly brought about by his disclosure about Rasim's death. What a gap his friend's death must have left in his life. And, knowing his history—who could blame him for associating love with loss or betrayal and never wanting to associate himself with it again?

She had wanted to comfort him, but Kadir didn't want her comfort. Sexual satisfaction seemed to be his only goal.

She swallowed.

Sometimes she thought…

She bit her lip, reluctant to acknowledge the thought which would never quite leave the edges of her mind. Because what if the once celibate Sheikh was using his newly discovered erotic skills to make her compliant? To *subdue* her and win her over—to make her fall in with whatever plans he had for Cameron?

Well, she couldn't ignore the topic for ever, and the longer it went on, the harder it would be for her to break away from him. He had carelessly mentioned 'a few weeks' at the beginning of their stay, and that time was fast approaching. Maybe it was time she exerted a little control of her own.

Before she got in too deep to tear herself away.

She moved out from behind the mosaic pillar and wandered down to the edge of the pool and Cameron immediately dived beneath the surface to repeat his underwater width.

'Did you see me, Mummy?' he spluttered as he emerged from the water and shook tiny droplets of water from his plastered black head. 'Was that good?'

'I did see you and it was brilliant! You swim like a wee eel!'

'Do I?'

'Yes!' She lifted him from the pool and wrapped a towel around him, her fingers wiggling mischievously beneath his arms. 'And you're just as slippery!'

He giggled as she tickled him and she wondered how she could ever take him away from all this... this *ease* and privilege. Would he resent her if she did so? Her introspection was halted by Morag bustling in to supervise the dressing of her young charge before taking him away for lunch, leaving Caitlin alone with Kadir.

She had seen him naked many times, but that had always been within the closeted privacy of the bedroom. Right now it seemed surreal to see the desert King half submerged in the turquoise water, his muscular weight resting on his elbows as he leaned on the side of the pool and studied her. His black hair lay flat against his head and against the olive-skinned wetness of his face, his ebony eyes gleamed like dark jewels. And, oh, didn't her heart and her body just clench with hopeless and instinctive longing?

'Such a pity you can't come in and join me,' he

murmured. 'Think what fun we could have together in the water.'

'You may be trying to propel Xulhabi into a new age of enlightenment, but I really don't think the palace is ready for mixed bathing at this stage.'

'I make the laws, Caitlin.'

'But there are servants everywhere,' she continued, dismissing his arrogant boast with the ghost of a smile. 'It wouldn't be appropriate, even if we *were* the kind of couple who messed around during daylight hours, which we aren't. And besides, I need to talk to you.'

Kadir hauled himself out of the pool, noting the way her body instinctively tensed as he moved closer. Her awareness of him was always apparent and he knew if he laid one finger on her, she would start to fall apart in his arms, just as she always did. Yet the expression on her face suggested that sex was the last thing on her mind right now—and the new-found glint of determination he could read in those ice blue eyes made him wary.

'What do you want to talk to me about?' he questioned, holding out a hand so that a servant immediately appeared with a white towelling gown, which Kadir shrugged on over his wet shoulders.

She didn't answer until he had belted up the robe and the servant had scurried away. 'I'm not sure that now is the ideal time to be having this conversation,' she prevaricated.

'Tell me,' he commanded imperiously.

She met his gaze and drew in a deep breath. 'You must know we can't stay here indefinitely like this, Kadir. We still haven't set out any timeline for our departure and it's not fair on Morag.'

'Has Morag expressed any desire to leave?'

'Well, no. But that's not the point. She's probably just being polite.'

'You don't think it might have something to do with the friendship she has struck up with my head groom, Ghassan, which is leading her to spend so much time in the stables when she isn't caring for our son? Either that, or she's showing a late-onset interest in riding, which I somehow doubt.'

'The fact that Morag is using her time wisely is irrelevant,' she shot back. 'I happen to have some commitments of my own back in Scotland.'

He raised his eyebrows. 'What kind of commitments?'

'I have a job, in case you'd forgotten. I'm a photographer and there's a backlog of photos I'm due to take, which need to be made into greeting cards before Christmas.'

'And the entire western world will grind to a halt if these greetings cards aren't made available?'

'Don't you *dare* patronise me, Kadir Al Marara!' she returned heatedly. 'I *need* to work! I've always worked—even though my earnings were never destined to break the bank. *You* may have been born with a silver spoon in your mouth, but not all of us have had your advantages.'

There was a pause during which Kadir found himself considering what his life might have been like if he had been given the birthright of most men and the weight of his destiny had not been quite so heavy. If he had been forced to work simply to put bread in his mouth. Hadn't that been his fantasy as a child? Sometimes a royal procession would travel to Azraq and, from within the sumptuous splendour of his golden carriage, he had observed the ragged street urchins playing in the dust, and had envied them. While most boys had longed to be kings or princes, he had simply yearned to be ordinary. 'None of us has any control over the circumstances of our birth,' he observed wryly. 'We can only hope to influence what happens to us later.'

'Yes, I realise that. But you're skating round the subject, as well you know, and you can't keep ignoring it for ever. I want to go home, Kadir.'

'Do you?' he demanded.

'This isn't real,' she breathed. 'It doesn't feel real. It's like I'm living in some kind of limbo.'

Kadir felt his breath catch as her stark words took root and he realised he had been burying his head in the sand—which was all very well for ostriches, but not kings of the desert. He had been aware for days that this clandestine affair of theirs could not continue indefinitely, and that the problem was only going to get worse if he kept pushing it to the back of his mind.

Wasn't it time that he bit the bullet and did what he needed to do, even though he had once sworn that he would never go through with this particular measure again? He had vowed never to let another person get too close to him, but he could see that, with Caitlin, he was going to have his work cut out to maintain that state of affairs.

'I need to talk to you, too. But not now and not here,' he said, gesturing towards his wet hair. 'I must first dry off and get changed but also, what I am about to say to you requires a certain degree of formality.'

'Oh?' Her brow pleated into a frown. 'Now you're talking in riddles.'

'Or perhaps simply stirring your interest? It seems to have worked, in any case.' Briefly, he lifted a hand to summon an aide, who came scurrying towards him. 'Come to my office in an hour, Caitlin.' His eyes glittered. 'I think you know the way well enough by now. I have a business proposition to put to you.'

CHAPTER ELEVEN

'WILL YOU MARRY me, Caitlin?'

Despite the generous proportions of the Sheikh's office, Caitlin felt the walls closing in on her as she stared in disbelief at the robed figure seated behind the desk who was studying her with an expression of amused speculation—as if her open-mouthed reaction was the last thing he had been expecting.

'You look shocked,' he observed, when still she said nothing.

Caitlin shook her head as she tried to absorb the enormity of the words Kadir had just uttered, but it was difficult to take it all in. She touched the polished wood of the desk—not touching it for luck but checking it was real—to reassure herself that she wasn't dreaming. 'Of course, I'm shocked.'

His eyes narrowed. 'But surely you must have considered that marriage might be an option at some point?'

Again, she shook her head, disbelief rippling through her as she stared at the desert King who'd just proposed marriage in the most unromantic of circumstances. There had been no moonlight or champagne and he certainly hadn't dropped down onto bended knee. His hair still damp from swimming, the Sheikh of Xulhabi had just asked Caitlin Fraser to be his bride, a proposition which once would have filled her with giddy delight. But delivered in the emotionless style of someone who was reading from a shopping list—even though he probably didn't even know what a shopping list was—Kadir's proposal had filled her with nothing but distrust.

But *he* was the one who had described it as a 'business proposition'. *He* wasn't building it up to be something it wasn't, was he? So maybe that was the way she ought to regard it, too.

'No,' she replied slowly. 'I can honestly say it hadn't crossed my mind that you might ask me to marry you.'

He leaned back in a highly embellished chair. 'And what do you say, now I have?'

She shrugged as she looked around the room. Golden pens were gleaming in a jewelled container in front of him and all the inlaid furniture was incredibly beautiful, but suddenly everything in the room seemed very foreign to her. Which was exactly how she felt. Foreign and alone. Like someone auditioning for a role which was never going to be right for her. 'I don't know,' she said, at last. 'What would happen, if I said yes?'

'It's very straightforward. You would be my Queen and my consort. Traditionally, such a position is a springboard for charitable works and, of course, we have the resources to make that possible. You would have your own staff. You could run your office as you see fit, for I am aware that as an independent woman—'

'Are you being sarcastic?' she questioned suspiciously.

He shook his head. 'Not at all. I am trying to make…*allowances*, Caitlin—something which I am not normally required to do. I am aware that you have a career and that perhaps…' He held out his palms in an expansive gesture she had seen him use before. 'Perhaps you might wish to continue with that career, although on a much smaller scale, of course.'

'Like how?'

'Well, it wouldn't be appropriate for you to produce Christmas cards in a country which doesn't actually celebrate that particular holiday, but there's no reason why you couldn't do some work for the Xulhabian tourist board. We're hoping to expand the travel industry and to encourage visitors in the near future and you could help promote that.'

'Wow.' She expelled a slow breath of air. 'You've got it all worked out, haven't you?'

'I have done my best to come up with a solution to our…dilemma,' he said, flicking her a shuttered black gaze. 'So what do you say, Caitlin? Is this something which might appeal to you?'

Caitlin didn't answer immediately, mainly because her thoughts were still in such a muddle. Was it typical of *all* men or just this man—that they could address all the practical concerns of an unexpected proposal of marriage, without even touching on the emotional ones? 'I don't know,' she admitted. 'Your reasons are—'

'Logical?' he supplied as he plucked one of the golden pens from the container and began to twirl it in between his thumb and forefinger. 'And lucid? Both qualities which should never be underestimated. Think about it, Caitlin, and then ask yourself, why *wouldn't* we marry? We share a son—a fine boy who will one day be King. Wouldn't parents who are wed make life so much easier for him?'

'I suppose so,' she admitted.

'He likes being here in the palace,' he continued. 'Anyone can see that. And all the time he is learning. About horses and falcons and history. About the history of Xulhabi, which will be invaluable to his future.' He paused. 'You must realise that I can offer him the finest tutors—'

'But,' she put in, like a drowning woman attempting to cling to the raft of her old life, 'I've got him down for an infant school on the mainland starting next September.

Their eyes met. 'That's not going to happen,' he said quietly. 'You must have realised that by now. Because not only do I need to marry in order to legitimise my succession, there is also the thorny subject of Cameron's security if you were to return to Scotland.'

Caitlin flinched, because those particular words struck home. Several times she'd thought what might happen if she insisted on taking Cameron back—then letting him come out to visit his father on high days and holidays. Mightn't Cameron start resenting the laughable contrast between life as a desert prince and life as an ordinary Scottish schoolboy? And what *of* the security aspect? No matter how much protection Kadir paid for, wouldn't she be forever looking over her shoulder? Jumping at every unexpected sound and terrified someone would snatch away her beloved boy?

'I can understand perfectly the reasons why you've asked me to marry you,' she said slowly. 'But you've made no mention of *us* in all this.'

'Us?' he said, as if she had just uttered a word he couldn't comprehend.

'About…about what it would be like for us to be man and wife.'

'I think we could coexist quite—'

'Happily?' she inserted sarcastically.

'Certainly without rancour,' he amended coolly. 'Neither of us seem to have had any complaints about the physical side of our relationship and I see no reason why that shouldn't continue.'

'Is that why you seduced me, Kadir?' she questioned suddenly. 'To lull me into a state of blissful dependence, knowing that one day it might serve you well?'

There was a pause. A pause which seemed to go on as his eyes just got blacker and blacker—unless you counted the furnace-bright spark at their centre. 'I seduced you because I couldn't get you out of my mind,' he husked at last. 'Because you were like a fire in my blood which would not be doused. You still are. Because no matter how often I feed my hunger for you, it still returns—even stronger than before.' He slammed the pen down onto the desk and stared at her. 'Is that what you wanted to hear, Caitlin?'

It was the most passionate thing he'd ever said and, almost without thinking, Caitlin placed her hand over the sudden jump of her heart before quickly letting it fall back down onto her lap. But he must have seen the gesture and correctly interpreted it because his eyes suddenly lost their blazing centre and became flat—almost matt.

'But that is simply passion—or lust, depending on your definition. And if you're holding out for love—if that's what all this is about,' he added softly, 'then that I cannot do. This proposal comes unencumbered by any false promises, which will leave you permanently disappointed. Do you understand what I'm saying to you?'

And the weirdest thing was that Caitlin *could* understand. Now that he'd told her more about himself and she had pieced together some of the fragments of his past, she'd been able to work out some of the things which motivated this battle-scarred man. Born into a dysfunctional relationship which hadn't worked on any level, he had pointed the finger of blame towards the unpredictability of emotion. He had considered his father a fool because he'd married for love, rather than duty, which was why he'd made duty his priority for his own wedding to Adiya.

But in the end, both duty *and* love had let him down—no wonder he was wary about relationships.

Yet with Cameron...

Caitlin felt her throat dry, wanting to hide from the truth, but knowing she couldn't. Because the one bright element in this situation was watching Kadir's relationship with his son blossom. They had hit it off from the get-go and it had been a pretty amazing thing to observe. Couldn't the bond they shared be a new beginning, of sorts? Was it too much to hope that Kadir might come to trust those new feelings and spread them around, like the rays of light radiating from the sun?

Spread them to her?

Maybe. Maybe not. She certainly couldn't enter into marriage if her sole objective was to get Kadir to love her, because he had ruled that out most emphatically. But that didn't mean she couldn't lead by example, or that she couldn't hope things might one day change. Because how could a damaged man learn to love and trust unless he was shown the way? Couldn't she demonstrate that she was willing to forget the past and move on from it? That there was more to a relationship than the stuff which happened in the bedroom—no matter how mind-blowing the sex happened to be.

She wondered briefly if she should make him wait. Play power games designed to show him she wasn't a total pushover. But what would be the point of that? They'd start trying to score points off each other and the truth would disappear and all you'd be left with would be a couple of egos, battling for supremacy. And that was the last thing any of them needed.

So she pinned a smile to her lips and, to her surprise, her answer came easily. 'Yes, Kadir,' she said softly. 'I will marry you.'

'Good.' For a long moment he studied her before rising up from behind the desk and walking over to the window, where he floated down the blinds, just as he had done once before. 'I believe it is tradition at this stage to kiss,' he said softly as

he began to move towards her and she could feel
an instant rush of heat.

His lips were hard but his kiss was sweet and
with very few preliminaries he was rucking up
her tunic with hands which were trembling—but
weren't hers trembling, too? He trickled his fin-
gertip over the goosebumps which iced her thighs
and as Caitlin squirmed ecstatically, he kissed her
again. Seamlessly, he slid down her panties and laid
her on the silken surface of the Persian carpet and
it felt like a dream. The most delicious dream she'd
ever had. Chandeliers and golden vaulted ceilings
shimmered above them as Kadir lifted his robes
to straddle her.

Yet despite being more turned on than she could
ever remember, Caitlin felt a rush of emotion as
she looked up into his shuttered face and lifted her
trembling fingertips to the rough shadow at his jaw.
Her body clenched around him as he made that first
thrust and she breathed out a sigh of pleasure as he
began to move. He was so big and so powerful—
and the feeling was so incredible that for a moment
she felt dangerously close to tears.

And right then all her wasted emotions were replaced by pure sensation as he silenced her cries
of pleasure with his lips. Her orgasm was spiral-
ling up inside her—so fast and perfect and inevitable. It slammed through her with such force that
her head fell back against the rug and then Kadir

began to come himself, his shuddered words soft, yet fractured.

For a long while afterwards she didn't speak. She didn't want to shatter the magic of the moment. But then dark realisation intruded and, insistently, she shook his shoulder. 'Kadir. Don't go to sleep.'

He opened his eyes. 'What is it?'

'You didn't use any protection.'

'No,' he said, frowning. 'There wasn't time and I wasn't thinking straight. Neither were you, or you would have reminded me.'

She sat up, raking her fingers through her tousled hair. 'And that's all it was—a momentary lapse caused by passion?'

Kadir considered her words. She had insisted that lies were a waste of time, and surely one of the perks of a situation like theirs was that you could afford to be honest. They weren't pretending to be in love. They weren't striving for the impossible goals which people chased and then felt shortchanged when they didn't materialise.

'No, maybe that's not all,' he admitted slowly. 'You are going to be my wife and I want the wedding to happen as soon as possible. Would it really make a big difference if you fell pregnant in the meantime?'

'If I *fell pregnant in the meantime*?' she echoed. Furiously, she reached for her discarded underwear. 'We haven't even *discussed* having another baby!'

'But the main purpose of marriage is for procreation, surely. You want to give Cameron brothers and sisters, don't you, Caitlin?'

'That's not the point!' she hissed.

'Why not?'

'Why not?' She jumped to her feet, slithering back into her panties. 'You bang on about me being an independent woman—but you're only paying lip service to it, aren't you, Kadir? You say I can "do some work" for the Xulhabian tourist board, yet at the first opportunity you forget to use a condom!' She drew in a deep breath. 'Admittedly, I got carried away myself, and therefore I'm as much to blame as you for what just happened, but even so—you can't just make out like it doesn't *matter.*'

'Caitlin—' he said, rising to his feet.

'Don't you "Caitlin" me! Either you can see that what we just did was a big mistake, or already we're in trouble.'

He drew in a deep breath, wishing he could brush the subject aside, but he recognised that she had a point. And it might be sensible to acknowledge that.

'I was wrong,' he admitted bluntly. 'My actions were not premeditated and I wasn't thinking straight. But in future I will make no such assumptions and we will add to our family only after mutual agreement, if at all. Does that satisfy you?'

'I suppose so.'

'So why don't we turn our attention to something which is guaranteed to make you smile again?'

'What is it?' she questioned, not bothering to keep the sulk from her voice.

He picked up a previously unnoticed small leather box which was lying on his desk, flipping it open to reveal a huge diamond ring resting against a bed of dark velvet. The stone's many facets sent out astonishing rays of rainbow light and it was undoubtedly the brightest thing in an already bright room. 'Go on,' he said, handing it to her. 'Try it on.'

Caitlin lifted the ring from the box. She could tell he was making an effort and he was looking at her with an expression of quiet satisfaction, as though no woman could fail to love such an enormous rock. But all she could feel was the heavy weight of the cold stone. It was too big for her finger. Too big for any finger, really. It occurred to her that she might have liked it better if he'd slipped it on her hand himself. 'It's beautiful,' she said dutifully.

'It's thirty-two carats,' he murmured.

To Caitlin this piece of information meant precisely nothing. The only carrot she was familiar with was the kind she secretly blitzed into a tomato sauce as she endeavoured to get Cameron to eat more vegetables.

And suddenly she felt an unbearable wave of nostalgia for those simple days she suddenly realised would never come again.

CHAPTER TWELVE

SHE HAD A crown containing the biggest emerald in the world.

She wore glittering diamonds in her hair.

And a fitted golden wedding dress embroidered with thousands of tiny seed pearls, which gleamed milky and soft beneath the fretwork of lights in the palace ballroom. In fact, Caitlin was wearing so much precious finery she could barely move, and each time she did something jangled, leaving her feeling a bit like Tinkerbell. Thank goodness the bride's walk towards the groom was traditionally slow, because she certainly couldn't have managed it any faster. Yet, despite the circumstances which had brought her to this place, her stately passage towards her future husband had felt bright and magical and full of possibilities. Since the royal announcement of their wedding had ricocheted around the globe, Caitlin had clung to those feelings of hope and joy, holding them close to her like a talisman.

'You look beautiful, Mama.'

The voice of her son butted into her thoughts and Caitlin looked down at a barely recognisable Cameron, clad in matching cloth of gold for his role as attendant to the bride. Some time during the last couple of weeks he had started substituting 'Mummy' and 'Daddy' with 'Mama' and 'Papa', and she wondered if he'd learnt to do that during one of the royalty etiquette classes he had shared with his father.

'Just like a queen!' Cameron added, with a gap-toothed grin.

'That's because your mother *is* a queen now,' said Kadir softly. 'And you, my son, are a prince of the desert.'

'*Am* I?'

'You most certainly are. And when Mama and I have returned from our honeymoon in the desert, you and I are going riding together as all princes should.'

'On my new horse?'

Kadir smiled. 'On your new horse, yes. So you must think about what you'd like to call him and be very good for Morag while we're away. Will you promise me you'll do that?'

'Oh, yes, Papa. I will.'

On cue, Morag stepped forward to take Cameron's hand and as Caitlin watched him trotting away happily at his nanny's side, she felt a weird twist of emotion—realising that this was the first time she'd ever spent a night apart from her little boy. Knowing that this was the first of many partings as the years took him towards adulthood. As he disappeared from view, she looked up to find Kadir's black eyes studying her.

'You'll miss him?' he questioned.

His perception startled her. 'Yes.'

'You're a good mother, Caitlin,' he said suddenly.

And that felt like the greatest compliment he could ever pay her. Better than telling her that her lips were soft or her hair like fire. Full of unexpressed emotion, she nodded. 'Thank you.'

She was glad the day was almost over. There had been so many things to organise in this new country which was now her home. Fittings for her elaborate gown and rubber-stamping the carefully worded statements which had been sent out by Kadir's office to the world's press. She'd been asked to approve menus and decide on flowers. And then had come the long ceremony involving much feasting and intricate musical performances, before the culmination of the event when they had recited solemn vows in Xulhabian, which had required a lot of heavy-duty prepping on her part. Now her hennaed finger sported a heavy wedding band of glittering emeralds and sapphires—the colours of the Xulhabian flag.

She'd even been having lessons in camel-riding—their intended mode of transport for the honeymoon. And then last night, when her nerves had been at their most frayed and she had longed for Kadir's embrace, tradition had reigned supreme and they had spent the night in separate beds, leaving her feeling slightly divorced from reality.

Divorce.

That was a word she probably shouldn't be using—not in any sense. Because she had been made to understand that any formal dissolution of the marriage would be highly undesirable. Kadir had said as much soon after she had accepted his proposal.

'I cannot fail this time, Caitlin.' His words had been heavy. 'And I cannot be seen to fail. The future of my country depends on stability and continuity.'

'Neither of us will fail at this.' Her own response had been fervent. She had meant every word. 'This is too important. For both of us. And for our son.'

The train of camels which was taking them to their desert destination was a throwback to earlier times, when such a mode of transport had been the only one available. She and Kadir each had a camel—hers was called Lutfi—with two bodyguards riding in front and behind. Servants had already been dispatched to the oasis where a camp had been set up and, just as the sun was sinking, they rode into the clearing, where a huge Bedouin tent awaited them. Outside, glowing lamps were already lit and, in the distance, someone was playing a musical instrument she didn't recognise, which sounded magical and enchanting.

In the distance, lush palm trees fringed a space of water and Caitlin sucked in a disbelieving breath as Kadir helped her down from her camel, as she witnessed the most stunning sunset she had ever seen. Celestial fire and flame were turning the sand blood-red and she could see touches of indigo and saffron bruising the edges of the sky.

'Oh, but it's beautiful,' she exclaimed.

And so was she, thought Kadir, as he watched her delicate features light up. He felt almost… *elated*—something rare enough to be remarkable. He had been taken aback by the fleeting sense of joy which had clutched at his heart during the ceremony—a strange reaction for someone who had vowed never to marry again. But he had put his reaction down to Cameron's presence by his mother's side and the pleasing fact that his country's succession was now assured. He'd convinced himself that his continuing contentment was due to nothing more complicated than paternal satisfaction and a sense of having got his own way—as well as anticipation about the wedding night ahead.

He glanced across at his bride.

Freed of her wedding attire, her fiery hair accentuated by the setting sun and her tunic billowing in the faint desert breeze, she looked almost at one with the land. Wild and carefree, her appearance touched something unknown and deep at the very core of him, which made his blood begin to pulse with honeyed sweetness. Breaking into a stream of rapid Xulhabian, he spoke to all the attendant staff—bodyguards included—who quickly began moving away from the proximity of the Bedouin tent.

'What did you say to them?' Caitlin asked, once they had all disappeared.

He lifted her up into his arms then, her hair flame-bright against the pale silk which covered his chest. 'I told them I wished to be alone with my new bride and they should not come near us again until I summon them,' he growled. 'Later, I will show you the stars in the heavens, which will be brighter than any stars you have ever seen. But in the meantime, I believe it is another of your British traditions to be carried over the threshold.'

'I believe it is,' she said, a smile curving her lips as he pushed back the canvas flap and dipped his head to carry her inside.

But to his pleasure—and his relief, for he was unbearably turned on—Caitlin didn't make any predictable comments about how deceptively large the tent was, nor did she coo or swoon over the luxurious brocades and silks which were scattered over the divans. She didn't even notice the large, beribboned box which sat on a small table beside the widest divan. Instead she was eagerly lifting her head for his kiss, her hands clutching at his shoulders as if she were feeling his body for the first time. And suddenly his hands were moving over her with equal impatience, as if it were an eternity since he had been intimate with her, rather than a single night. Their robes pooled to the ground and at last they were naked, their bodies illuminated by the fretwork flicker of the intricate lights which dangled from the ceiling.

Kadir gave a soft groan as he cupped the swell of her breast, revelling in the dark contrast of his fingers against her fair skin. 'I want you, my Queen,' he said, unsteadily. 'I wonder if you have any idea just how much?'

'K-Kadir.'

He didn't like it when she said his name like that—yet he liked it way too much. It sounded… He shook his head. It was hard to define because nobody had ever spoken to him that way before. As if his name were a prayer. Or a plea. But words didn't matter—not when she was doing something far more distracting. His mouth dried to dust because suddenly Caitlin was sliding to her knees before him, almost as if she were supplicating herself to him. But she wasn't. She was reaching between his thighs and curling her fingers around his arousal—an erotic and possessive cradling of his manhood. With her other hand she had begun playing with his balls and the sensation was so good it was almost unbearable…

'Caitlin!' He shuddered as she lowered her head onto his aching shaft, her tongue tantalising him with feather-light licks before she took him fully into her mouth. He clenched his fists and resisted the desire to close his eyes. It was certainly easier not to orgasm without any visual stimuli but it was also intensely erotic to watch the bobbing movement of her bright hair as she sucked on him. He wanted to tell her to stop and he wanted her to keep doing exactly what she was doing, but it was all pretty academic anyway because, no matter how long he tried to ward off the inevitable, he was soon jerking helplessly into her mouth, his fingers tangled in her hair as his seed spilled onto her lips.

For a long moment he felt completely defenceless—a sensation so disturbing that it threatened to eclipse the last sweet echoes of his orgasm. But as she raised her flushed face to his, he reasserted his mastery by lifting her up and carrying her over to the divan.

'That was…unexpected,' he observed, once she was prone on the golden sheet.

'I wanted to do something special for you.' She hesitated as he brushed his lips over her neck. 'To take the initiative for once, if you like. I mean, I know I've been involved in all the wedding planning, but sometimes this week I've felt a bit...'

The progress of his lips halted. 'A bit what?'

'Passive, I guess,' she admitted. 'As if I have no control over what is happening to me.'

'But isn't it sometimes a good thing, to feel passive?' he mused, his voice now muffled as he moved his mouth towards her belly. 'Like now, for example?'

'Oh, Kadir,' she breathed.

'You like that?'

'No, I'm hating every second of it. Can't you tell?'

He thought about tasting *her* until she was crying out beneath the quick flick of his tongue. But his current need was more basic than that. He just wanted to be inside her—and something about the elemental urgency of that need disturbed him.

This time there were plenty of condoms to hand and when he entered her—feeling as hard as he could ever remember—she came almost immediately, as if she had been teetering on the brink for too long. As her body spasmed around him Kadir felt the instant pump of his seed. And this time his orgasm seemed as if it were never going to end.

For a while they lay in silence until the hard pound of his heart slowed. Until the sweat which sheened his brow had begun to cool. He opened his eyes to find her looking at him and suddenly he wanted—no, *needed*—to assert his mastery. To feel more like the man he usually was, rather than someone who he was beginning not to recognise. Shaking off his inertia, he stirred.

'I've bought you a present,' he said. 'Look. It's right beside you.'

She turned her head and for the first time appeared to notice the fancy beribboned box lying there. 'Gosh,' she said, blinking very rapidly.

'Well, don't just stare at it. Open it.'

Caitlin began to untie the ribbon and pulled out a box from within the fancy paper. Inside was a camera. The kind of camera she'd always dreamed of owning but had never imagined she would. Top of the range and eye-wateringly expensive, she turned it round and round in her hands as if she couldn't quite believe she was holding it. But the gratitude which rushed over her was nothing to do with the money he must have spent—because when had anyone ever bought her a gift which felt so *right*? She felt the sudden unexpected prick of tears at the backs of her eyes. So *thoughtful*?

'Do you like it?'

Still overcome, she nodded.

'There's a printer to go with it back at the palace.'

She put the camera down and touched her fingers to the rough graze of his jaw. 'Thank you.'

'Just let one of my aides know if you need any

more accessories and they can get them for you.' He flickered her an indecipherable stare. 'Like I said, you'll need something to do alongside your charity work. Something which keeps you from getting bored, or from feeling quite so *passive*.'

She told herself it was only gentle mockery. That nobody would give you a beautiful gift one minute, then turn around and make a veiled criticism the next. But Caitlin realised that Kadir was doing that thing he always did straight after they'd had sex.

He was distancing himself.

CHAPTER THIRTEEN

COLD DREAD WAS mounting inside him as the plane began its final descent and Kadir stared out of the porthole window without really seeing anything.

He should be experiencing a sensation of quiet satisfaction. The honeymoon had been a success. Not even he, the world's greatest cynic, could deny that. It had been easy—ridiculously so. By day, he had shown his new bride the desert he knew so well, and by night they had enjoyed long feasts of the senses which had blown his mind. Caitlin had been thrilled by his wedding gift of a new camera, and he had watched her busily snapping images of the stark terrain whenever time allowed.

But now the honeymoon was over. He'd sent his servants back by camel train, while he and Caitlin had commandeered the royal flight. Any minute now they would be touching down at the royal palace and seeing their son after a week's absence. He couldn't have asked for a better outcome to the marriage he had so carefully engineered, and yet...

Yet…

Now he wondered if he had been incautious. If he had given too much of himself to his new bride and fed dreams he had not intended to feed. If he had let his guard down a little too often during the preceding week.

A sigh left his lips. He had a problem. A problem which could no longer be ignored, even though he'd been loath to address it. He certainly hadn't wanted to ruin their short honeymoon and he hadn't wanted to confront it in an environment where he would be unable to escape from his new wife.

A wife he suspected was falling in love with him.

He felt his mouth twist as familiar faint echoes of fear and cynicism washed over him in a dark tide. His own experience had fanned his determination to never fall victim to love's capricious wiles, but he had been on the receiving end of unwanted devotion often enough to recognise the telltale signs when he saw them. The tender eyes and lingering glances. The shy biting of the lips followed by a gentle smile.

Yet because he had never been intimate with anyone before Caitlin, the problem had only ever been academic. Women had adored him from afar. He had never put himself directly in the firing line before because he hadn't had to. He'd been able to walk away.

But he couldn't walk away from his new wife

and neither did he want to, because she came as part of a package and that package included his son. A son he needed to continue the Al Marara line for which he had worked so tirelessly.

His vision clearing a little, he stared down at the gleam of golden turrets as the jet circled the palace and a sense of resolve made him tighten his jaw. He liked Caitlin and enjoyed her company—he wasn't going to deny that. But that was all it could ever be. He wasn't going to start reaching for the stars, or reciting poetry to her. She was going to have to learn to manage her expectations. He didn't want her love distracting him and making demands on him. He didn't want to talk about *feelings*. He didn't want to engage in *any* kind of cloying emotional dependence. His jaw firmed. And as his wife, she needed to understand that.

'Are you looking forward to getting back?' he questioned, though from the brightness of her answering smile, you'd think he'd just lassoed the moon for her.

'Of course I am. I can't wait to see Cameron again. But I'm going to miss those nights, alone in the desert with you. And the days, come to think of it. I hope…' She hesitated, before reaching across to squeeze his hand. 'I hope things won't be terribly different when we're back at the palace.'

'I think it will be difficult to maintain that same level of intimacy,' he said, carefully removing his hand from hers. 'The nature of my work is such that I cannot guarantee being available for you with such frequency.'

'Oh.'

He flicked her a glance. 'But you understand what it's like, don't you, Caitlin? You understand the demands of my role?'

Caitlin forced herself to nod, telling herself that was what an understanding wife would do and that was what she was determined to be. The words she had spoken before and during the marriage ceremony she'd meant from the bottom of her heart. More than anything, she wanted to make this marriage of theirs work and the honeymoon had given her hope that such a thing was possible. A honeymoon which had been...

She leaned back against the comfy airline seat and sighed.

It had been magical; there was no other way to describe it. Totally and utterly magical. She had seen a much softer side to Kadir than he'd ever revealed to her before. During those hot, desert days and icy-cold nights some of the unremitting layers which could make him seem so unapproachable had been peeled away. Beneath a huge and silvery moon, she had caught glimpses of the man who had first stolen her heart.

He had taken her riding on one of the hardy Akhal-Teke horses which had accompanied them on the trip—just the two of them—his bodyguards keeping a discreet distance. He had shown her some of the secrets of the desert and the life which hummed beneath the seemingly unforgiving landscape. She had been remarkably un-spooked by the zig-zagging track of a sidewinder snake and had captured the slow progress of a desert tortoise with her camera. She remembered marvelling at the incredible *baswa* tree, which survived the barren conditions against all the odds, whose leaves could be boiled to make an invigorating tea and whose sap produced a delicious syrup.

And by night… Her heart pounded with erotic recall. Kadir was the most amazing lover—she'd known that before, of course, but somehow their marriage seemed to have strengthened the bond between them. At least, it had from her point of view. Sometimes when he was deep inside her, she wanted to cry because it was so beautiful. It was just like all those romantic novels and corny songs. It was like the first time she'd met him, only more so—because this time she knew him.

And she had fallen in love with him.

Was that so wrong? She stared down at her giant diamond ring, still glinting rather aggressively on her finger. How could it possibly be wrong, when he was her only lover and the father of her child? It wasn't as if she were demanding he love her back, because Kadir had told her he could never do that.

But she was convinced she could be contented with things as they stood, because she'd never felt this happy before. As if she were floating on air. As if she could conquer the world, if only the world would let her!

She turned to look at him, her gaze resting on his hawklike profile and the jet-darkness of his thick lashes. My husband, she thought lovingly. My brave and beautiful husband. 'Shall we have dinner tonight, as a family?' she asked.

He turned his head to meet her eyes and Caitlin wondered if she had imagined the sudden steely glint which had penetrated his his black gaze. For a minute he had looked... Her heart began to race with something which felt like fear. It was almost as if he were looking *through* her, rather than *at* her. As if the powerful connection which had existed between them all week had suddenly been snapped.

'I'm afraid that won't be possible,' he said, his apologetic shrug seeming a little half-hearted.

Caitlin was unable to keep the disappointment from her voice. 'Oh?'

'I must meet with my advisors after so long away. Naturally, I'll come and say hello to Cameron as soon as we arrive and spend some time with him, but after that you will have to excuse me.'

She waited for the placating kiss, for the smile which would reassure her that nothing had changed, but neither of these things happened and as the plane touched down she couldn't shake off her faint feeling of panic.

And wasn't it funny how panic could grow? A bit like a blemish on your face which nobody else could really see, only you kept touching it and touching it until suddenly it was livid and red and enormous. Because that was how it was with them. That was what her relationship with Kadir suddenly became. One minute she'd been kissing him beneath a canopy of stars—and the next she was left wondering whether the whole honeymoon had been as insubstantial as a desert mirage.

She tried her best to be pragmatic. She told herself that maybe her expectations had been unrealistically heightened by the emotion of the wedding, and she must be prepared to accept a less heady lifestyle now they were back in the palace. But even before their honeymoon, Kadir used to spend every night in her bed, even if he *had* slipped away before the rest of the palace had woken up. Whereas now he was absent for one, sometimes two nights in a row. He'd been busy with work, he said. He was making up for lost time, he said. And there was plenty of space for him to sleep in his office. Even though they had their own enormous section of the palace, she sometimes awoke in the lonely hours before dawn to find the space beside her still empty.

She tried to reassure herself about that too— because when he *was* in bed with her, it was as heart-stoppingly good as it had been before. And if she thought that sometimes he was only pretending to be asleep—well, that was just her imagination, wasn't it?

Wasn't it?

At least the Sheikh's attentions towards their son remained constant and Caitlin was able to derive comfort from that. Each morning she joined them in the stables and watched as their son grew more confident on his new pony—now called Bunni, which apparently meant brown and had nothing to do with rabbits.

With her new camera, she took hundreds of photos of Cameron with his father but she captured plenty of other images, too. Arty pictures of gilded arches, the misty blur of a fountain glimpsed through a curtain of flowers—and the snow-capped peaks of the Zeitian mountains. One shot she was particularly proud of—taken of Kadir as he walked through the wide palace corridors, his shoulders appearing to carry the weight of his destiny.

But these creative endeavours only went so far in providing her with a feeling of satisfaction, before her thoughts inevitably ran into the brick wall of fear. With each day that passed, it became harder to deny the sense of being the outsider in this gilded new home of hers. She became more and more certain that Kadir was pushing her away from him and one morning, her worst fears were confirmed.

Imagining her husband to still be occupied with the visiting Maraban Ambassador, Caitlin had been in her husband's office, a room to which, as Queen, she now had unfettered access. The light in there was particularly good and she wanted a shot of the rose garden before the sun was too high.

She wasn't snooping. Most definitely she wasn't snooping. She just happened to be walking past his desk. And what would anyone else do in the circumstances if they saw their own name on a sheet of paper, which was lying right next to a golden-framed photo of Cameron?

Without touching it, she quickly scanned the handwritten note, which had the name of a London legal firm embellished on the top. She remembered Kadir once telling her that all legal matters were conducted in English, because that meant they could be enshrined in international law and also because not many people spoke Xulhabian. It had made perfect sense at the time and Caitlin supposed she should be glad of it now because it meant she could understand what she was reading, but she almost wished she *didn't* understand. Her disbelieving mind skated past the formal greeting of 'Majesty' as she tried to absorb some of the letter's contents, because it was about her. Or, more specifically, it was about Cameron. Her throat felt raw and her eyes burned as one sentence branded itself on her brain and, despite its stuffy legal phraseology, it was easy to understand.

The marriage obviously confers legitimacy and inheritance rights on the young Prince, but also the mother will now be unable legally to remove the child from Xulhabi without your consent.

Suddenly it all made sense. The softening of Kadir's attitude towards her and the clever wooing. The way he'd made her *feel* stuff she'd never been expecting to feel. The sense that something tangible and wonderful had been within her reach, only to have it snatched away at the last moment. Caitlin's fingers tightened around her new camera. She wanted to hurl the expensive piece of kit to the ground and smash her foot down on it, but that would be the behaviour of a hysteric and she needed to be calm. Because everything she held dear depended on staying in control. She sank down on the window seat as she forced herself to focus on one single, comforting fact.

She wasn't going mad.

She wasn't imagining things which weren't really happening. She *was* being excluded! She had served her purpose by marrying the powerful Sheikh and, in so doing, had relinquished all her maternal authority, without her knowledge. How sneaky and cruel was that? Was that why he was pushing her further away from him—so that she could quietly be siphoned out of royal life? Perhaps that was the reason he'd been so keen to make their family bigger—also without her permission—so she could become some little breeding machine in the corner of the palace, quietly giving birth to heirs and spares.

And all the time she had been falling in love with him. Deeper and deeper and deeper. Did that make her as foolish as her poor mother had been? A deluded woman who had clung to the futile hope her married lover would one day leave his wife— and who had wasted so much time in pursuit of her own desires she had made her and Caitlin's lives a misery.

But she had been guilty of something similar. She had craved love from a man who had told her right from the beginning that he was unable to provide it. She had allowed her own romantic fantasies to blind her to a truth she had refused to recognise, which was that she was simply a means to an end. She'd been so grateful to him for providing her with security and for legitimising their son that she hadn't stopped to realise that she was never intended to be anywhere except on the sidelines.

As the sun rose higher in the sky behind her, she sat on the window seat and waited, her heart pounding a fast and steady beat as a feeling of doom threatened to envelop her.

She shook her head when a servant entered and enquired whether she required refreshments and she was equally negative when Makim appeared at the door to ask whether she was okay.

'I'm waiting for…' she nearly said *my husband*, until a small voice in her head suggested she might want to start recalibrating her mindset '…the Sheikh,' she finished, unable to keep a note of venom from her voice as she looked up defiantly at Kadir's aide.

'But have you not consulted with his diary, My Queen?' He seemed perplexed. 'His Serene Majesty has meetings until early this afternoon.'

'I don't mind. I'll wait.'

Had Kadir been alerted to this display of his wife's stubborn tenure? Was that why he appeared within minutes with an expression of irritation he didn't bother to hide.

'I'm assuming this is important?' he questioned.

For a moment Caitlin felt almost awestruck by his arrogance until she remembered that he was a master of battle—and didn't people say the best form of defence was attack? Well, maybe she would take their advice.

She got up from the seat and walked over to his desk, plucking up the lawyer's letter which was lying there.

'I've just read this!'

'Oh?' His features remained implacable. 'Have you been spying on me, Caitlin?'

'Don't you dare try to turn this round!' She sucked in a furious breath, waving the letter in front of him. 'Instead, why don't you try explaining *this*?'

It occurred to Kadir that never had anyone addressed him quite so insolently just as it occurred to him that maybe, in some mysterious way, he was relieved this had happened. At least now matters could be brought to a head and there could be no misunderstanding. 'What you read is nothing but the truth, Caitlin. There is really no need to distress yourself,' he said. 'You must have known deep down that such a clause would exist. Are there not laws in place in most countries, to prevent one parent fleeing with a child without permission? And when that child is a prince, it becomes even more important.'

'You think that's what I might do?'

Kadir met her eyes and suddenly the atmosphere between them changed. He felt the first fraught dark charge of something he didn't recognise and realised too late that, by bringing matters to a head, he was going to have to face the very truth he had been seeking to avoid. 'I don't know what you might do, Caitlin,' he answered quietly. 'I've always found women extremely unpredictable.'

She nodded as she stared into his eyes and then she began to speak.

'I thought I could be happy here,' she said slowly. 'Because there's pretty much everything here a person could ever want. I liked the way Cameron settled in here and I liked the way you interacted with him. I still do. And I like Xulhabi. The desert and the palace and the rose gardens. The capital city is buzzy and vibrant—what little I've seen of it—and I was looking forward to exploring more of the country as your Queen and taking on some charities of my own.'

'So there's no problem?' he said, coolly clipping out the words as if he were in a meeting with one of his diplomats.

She gave him a look—a look of such pain that it made him want to turn away. But he couldn't. He had to face this head-on because he owed it to her. And he owed it to Cameron, too.

'I think you'll find there is,' she said quietly. 'And you know exactly what it is.'

He knew what she meant. Of course he did. But surely it was her place to admit it, rather than his to accuse. Yet the very terms he was using disturbed him. *Admit. Accuse.* Weren't those words frequently used in a court of law? Not those usually associated with the subject they were talking about, even though neither of them had had the guts to mention it. Until now.

'You're in love with me?' he suggested.

Caitlin met the gleam of his black eyes without flinching, wishing she could deny his words, but she couldn't. And what would be the point of adding a layer of lies to this already heartbreaking situation?

'Yes, I'm in love with you,' she burst out. 'I know it's irrational and a complete waste of time, but there's nothing I can seem to do about it. I tried to forget you right from the start, but I couldn't. And when you found us, I tried to hate you for kidnapping us and bringing us here, but the terrible truth is that I actually liked it. In some warped kind of way I felt protected for the first time in my life. And I liked being with you again—'

'Caitlin—'

'No,' she interrupted fiercely. 'Let me finish this—because you were the one who asked the question and you are the one who needs to hear my answer. Maybe I'm one of those sad women who are programmed to care only for men who are cruel, just like my mother. Except that sometimes—when you forget to erect all those barriers around you—you aren't cruel at all. You're funny and clever and perceptive—which goes some way towards cancelling out your arrogance and high-handedness. I know. I should have had the courage to say all this to you before, but I didn't.' She gave a bitter laugh. 'Because when you asked me to marry you, I felt hope—I'm not going to deny that. I thought that, despite everything you'd said, you might be open to change. And then I thought we'd grown super-close over our honeymoon and we might continue to do so. I thought you might be willing to give us a chance—to see if that bond between us could grow.'

'Despite the fact I expressly told you that would never happen?' he demanded.

'Yes, despite all that,' she agreed. 'Delusional of me, I know—but hope can be an annoying thing and you can't always quash it, no matter how much you might try. But you began to do the exact opposite of getting closer, didn't you, Kadir? You began to push me away and that made me re-examine my own intentions. I'd been so sure that I could be contented with the very minimum of what most people ask in a marriage. But I've discovered I can't do that,' she finished huskily. 'I can't pretend things I don't feel, and I don't want my son to grow up in an atmosphere where he's afraid to show love, brought up by parents who are cold and distant with each other. If we do that, aren't we only perpetrating the kind of dysfunctional behaviour which made your own childhood so unhappy?'

'So what are you telling me, Caitlin?' he questioned harshly. 'What is your conclusion to this astonishing list of insights?'

Perhaps if he'd been a little kinder towards her,

then Caitlin might have backtracked a little. Might have suggested that maybe they should give it a month or two and see how things progressed. But the condemnation which glittered from his black eyes told her more than she could bear. And if he didn't love her now, in this early stage of their marriage, wasn't it inevitable that his feelings for her would turn at best to indifference and at worst to hate?

'I want to take Cameron back to Scotland with me,' she said, resolutely ignoring his hissed intake of breath. 'I know it won't be easy and I'm happy to take any recommendations you may have regarding security aspects—'

'Oh, *are* you?'

'He can come out here on a regular basis and, whenever you come to the UK, you can see him,' she continued. 'Because I will never deny you access.'

He met her eyes. 'But you are now aware that you cannot remove our son from the country without my permission,' he said quietly.

'Yes, I'm aware of that. But I'm hoping that you will be big enough to disregard that clause. You can have Cameron as often as is possible, but I'm asking you to let me take him back to Scotland. Please. Don't trap me here as if I were a butterfly in a jam jar.'

For a moment there was silence. A silence so

fragile yet so hefty that it seemed to bear down on Kadir like the crushing of a thousand trees on his shoulders. He saw her lips trembling, but for once they were not trembling with desire, but with apprehension. He knew he could insist that she stay and that the law was on his side. Given time, he might even be able to kiss her into something approaching submission—but that would be despicable. Because he had been honest with her, yes, but that honesty had destroyed something between them, and that something was trust. She was looking at him now with such wariness and disappointment in her eyes that he felt as if he had taken something very beautiful within the palm of his hand and crushed it. The pain inside him built and built. Any minute now and it would fell him completely.

'Take him,' he said heavily. 'Take Cameron back to Cronarty, but do it as quickly as possible. And now go, Caitlin. Leave me—not in peace, no—but at least with the time to compose myself before my next meeting.'

CHAPTER FOURTEEN

THE PAIN WAS still intense. Like an iron fist clamped around a raw and bloody heart, and Kadir had never known pain like it. Not during the many battles he had fought for his country, when his lifeblood had turned the sand rusty, or the witnessing of his friend's death. Not even during his mother's early rejection, or the subsequent discovery of his first wife's hopeless addiction. Because this pain was different. This was something else.

Standing in the palace courtyard, he stared up at the cloudless sky and watched the blue and green royal jet as it headed westward—towards Scotland and a tiny rain-lashed island. He bit down hard on his lip in an attempt to distract himself from the confusion of his thoughts and the disorientating feeling that his world was spinning out of control. He told himself that of *course* he would feel something when, just an hour earlier, he had said goodbye to his wife and son. But stupidly—and infuriatingly—he found himself having to blink back tears. Tears! He who had never cried in his life. Not even over Rasim. But then he'd never had to endure a farewell quite like this before.

Cameron had clung to him as if he never wanted to let him go, but children were capricious beings and one murmured mention from Morag about the pet hamster which awaited him back in Scotland had been enough to ensure an instant gap-toothed smile.

'I will come and meet Hamish very soon,' Kadir had said gravely.

'When, Papa?'

Kadir's eyes had met Caitlin's over their son's head and he had found himself wondering when those wide blue orbs had become such cold, pale ice. He had wanted to reach for her then and to hold her against the painful acceleration of his heart, but she had turned away, her expression tight and unmoving.

'As soon as it can be arranged,' he had replied, with forced jollity.

And now he was alone. Alone with his thoughts and all the freedom he had once craved. Freedom from the unrealistic and claustrophobic demands of something he had never asked for. He did not want her love—a love he was incapable of return-ing. And when she had told him she could not live that way he had let her go.

He had done the right thing by them all.

It was better this way.

He went to his office, but instead of distracting himself with the stack of paperwork which awaited his attention he found himself staring at the gold-framed photograph of his son, which Caitlin had taken. It had been shot soon after they had named Cameron's pony and it had been his son's first ride on Bunni. He had been beaming with pride and achievement and the look he had slanted at him had been all for his father. A look which had been conspiratorial and full of comradeship. And love.

And that was the photo which Caitlin had printed off and given to him in this golden frame. 'This is *my* wedding gift to *you*,' she had announced shyly.

He had felt choked—he wasn't going to deny that. And yet he had resented the way she'd forced him to feel that emotion. Had it been that which had made him nod his thanks and turn away in a manner which some people might have described as churlish?

Turning away from the window, he began to pace the room, wondering how he could bear to endure what he alone had orchestrated. Yet this was all for the best. Those were the words he kept repeating, like a mantra. If he kept telling himself it would be better for Caitlin and Cameron in the long run, then wouldn't that make his pain easier to bear?

But first he had to start believing it himself.

Sitting down behind his desk, he picked up his pen and pulled a sheet of paper towards him, not lifting his head or turning around to acknowledge the soft sound of the door opening behind him. Makim would quickly infer from his forbidding demeanour that he was not in the mood for conversation, or interruption. The way he felt right then, he couldn't imagine talking to anyone ever again.

He heard the sound of the door closing and still he ignored it.

'Kadir?'

It was a soft voice. A familiar voice. The voice which had murmured softly into his ear or cried out his name more times than he could bear to remember and Kadir cursed the tricks the mind could play. But he would not be haunted by her memory. He could not let himself do so—for that way lay madness.

'Kadir?'

The voice was a little louder now and Kadir froze, then turned round to see Caitlin standing there, still wearing the tweed skirt and blouse she had changed into before leaving for her flight.

Alarmed, he dropped his pen and rose to his feet, black fears like crows crowding swiftly into his mind. 'What's wrong?'

'Nothing's wrong.'

'Then…' He tensed, his eyes narrowing as he studied her face for clues. 'Why are you here?'

Why was she here? It was a question Caitlin had asked herself over and over during the drive back here and she still wasn't sure if she had come up with the right answer. The only thing she *had* known was that she couldn't go through with taking a sobbing little boy all the way back to Scotland. A little boy who had spent the entire journey to the airfield asking for 'Papa'. This might not be the best course of action—for her—but it was certainly the right thing for Cameron and she needed to cling on to that.

'I couldn't go through with it. I couldn't go back,' she said. 'Cameron was missing you so badly already. He didn't want to leave.'

'He didn't?'

The look of surprise and relief in his eyes was so raw that to see it felt as if she were invading a part of him he had never intended to show. And Caitlin realised then, as she had suspected all along, that Kadir *could* feel emotion. Just not for her. 'Mothers are supposed to put their children first,' she said. 'That's something my own mother never did for me, nor yours for you—and maybe it's time to redress that balance. I have to think about what Cameron needs—which is to stay here and grow up with you.'

'But I saw the royal jet flying westward.'

'I dispatched Makim to bring his hamster back

here. The air-conditioning in the palace means he should be fine.'

He was shaking his head. 'I don't understand.'

She could see that. It seemed she was going to have to spell it out for him.

'You told me you didn't do love, or, rather, that you *couldn't* do love. At first I didn't want to believe it because it didn't suit me, but gradually I came to accept that what you said was true. How could I fail to? You went out of your way to show me that you meant it. You made sure you pushed me away and kept me at arm's length. You rejected all my attempts to grow closer. After our honeymoon, it was like you shut down completely.'

'That much is true,' he said flatly.

It was a blank admission and one which sounded devoid of regret, but Caitlin hid her unrealistic sense of disappointment and continued.

'But you do love your son, don't you, Kadir? You love him so much that it's a gift to watch you together—it's *wondrous*. Yet you were prepared to let him go. You were prepared to sacrifice your own feelings to do what you felt was the best thing for Cameron—and me. And sacrifice is a form of love. In fact, it's possibly the greatest form of love there is, because it's totally lacking in ego, or self-interest.'

She swallowed back the tears which were welling up at the back of her eyes, because she didn't want to break down in front of him. There would be plenty of time for tears later.

'And that's why I've brought Cameron back to you.'

There was silence for a moment and his gaze was steady, as if he were giving her time to retract her statement, but when she said nothing, he spoke at last. 'And you?' he questioned heavily. 'What will you do?'

She shrugged. 'I will stay, because I have no choice other than to stay. I cannot deprive Cameron of a mother, any more than I can deprive him of a father. I will become the best Queen I can possibly be. I will accept and enjoy what is, and not yearn for things which are not mine to have. I will not ask you for love, Kadir, because one-sided love never really works—I saw that with my mother. And in time my feelings for you will fade—that's inevitable…a bit like the flowers in a hot summer garden wilting if they don't get enough water. All I ask is that you treat me with respect and set our son a good example of what an amicable relationship can be, so it doesn't put him off love and marriage when he is of an age to want those things for himself.' She forced a smile, which felt as if it were slicing her face in two. 'Let's do our best not to warp his perception about human relationships, shall we?'

Kadir closed his eyes, realising that she had condemned him with her words. That her generosity of spirit and good heart were making him feel like the most contemptible of men—and with good reason. He was not worthy of her. Perhaps he would never be worthy of her. But he had to show that he could try to be, if only she would give him one last chance. She had to. Because this was one battle he could not afford to lose. Unless it was already too late.

He opened his eyes and knew that he was responsible for the desperately sad expression she was doing her best to hide and a feeling of self-contempt made his blood run cold. What kind of brute was he? What *kind*?

He clenched his fists. 'Caitlin, I need to tell you something—'

'You don't—'

'Please. Hear me out, as I did you.' He sucked in a ragged breath. 'What I felt for you, all those years ago, was like a bolt of lightning to my heart. But my guilt about Adiya allowed me to convince myself it was nothing but the pent-up lust of a man who'd never had sex before, which had finally spilled over. Even when I returned to Scotland to find you again, I was certain that what I felt was nothing but carnal desire, and the anger I experienced when I found out about Cameron gave me permission to dislike you. But I couldn't dislike you. The more time I spent with you, the more I saw your humour and softness, which had so attracted me in the first place. I discovered what a good person you were—as well as being a remarkable mother to our son. And that frightened me.'

For the first time, her face lost some of its tight, pinched expression. 'Frightened you? You don't strike me as the kind of man who would be frightened of anything.'

'Everyone feels fear, Caitlin,' he said, and as he spoke he realised he was being truly honest with himself. 'It's just that some of us are better at hiding it than others. I never opened up to the pain I'd felt when I was a child. I'd never shown anyone how much my mother's treatment of me wounded me. I think I was trying to protect my father from any more suffering. He already had her betrayal to contend with—I think if he'd known of my heartbreak, it would have finished him.' He sucked in a shuddered sigh. 'Just like I never showed the pain I felt when Rasim died, for it felt like a kind of weakness to do so. I still had a country to repair after the ravages of war, and a people who were looking to me for guidance.'

'So you buried all those feelings deep inside you,' she said slowly. 'Which only made it worse. Because things which are buried just get more and more rotten.'

He gave a bitter laugh. 'You could say that.'

'But why are you telling me all this, Kadir?' she

said, her voice sounding very precise, as if she was picking out each word with care. 'And why now?'

Had he wanted her to guess at his reasons without having to articulate them? Of course he had. Because that would have been easier. Easier for him, certainly. But not for her. And he owed her this. He owed her so much, but this more than anything. 'Because the pain of not having you in my life is far greater than any other pain I could ever contemplate,' he husked. 'It eclipses everything—even the fear of rejection and of becoming too reliant on another human being and opening myself up to hurt again. I've discovered that holding back from you and pushing you away doesn't make me happy. Having you beside me does—but I've been fighting those feelings for so long.

'I fought them at the beginning and I did the same when I brought you here. I fought them on our honeymoon—the single most blissful week of my life. And now I fear it may be too late. That you may have given up on me. But I love you, Caitlin. I love you so much.' He slapped his hand over his heart and let it lie there. 'Believe me when I tell you that.'

Had he been hoping for instant capitulation? For her to fling herself into his arms and forgive him? Yes, he probably had. But she didn't move. She just stood there surveying him, with that same wary look in her eyes.

'You don't have to say all this stuff to seal the

deal, you know, Kadir,' she said stiffly. 'Cameron is coming to live here, no matter what.'

He shook his head. 'I'm not trying to seal the deal,' he said simply. 'I'm trying to heal the deal.'

Maybe it was the break in his voice which swung it—that or the transparent brightness of his gaze. Because suddenly she was hurling herself across the office as she had done once before on a plane high above the Alps. But this time she was not brandishing a jewelled paper knife above her head and threatening to do him harm. This time she was in his arms and covering his face with kiss after fervent kiss and telling him she loved him, that she had loved him from the first time she'd ever seen him and that she would never stop loving him.

And for the first time in Kadir's life he knew peace. Real peace. Solid and rich and beautiful. Because he didn't just love Caitlin—he believed her and he *trusted* her. And right now, that felt like the most profound gift he had ever received.

EPILOGUE

'MAGNIFICENT.'

'Superbly captured.'

'What talent! Honestly, I had no idea.'

Caitlin smiled. Some of the praise was in English and some in Xulhabian, but she couldn't fail to be aware that the reaction to her photographic exhibition remained heart-warmingly positive. It had been open for a month now but its sell-out status showed no sign of abating.

'If it was anyone else reaping this kind of praise, I'd be worried that their ego might start over-inflating,' Kadir murmured and she looked up to see a smile playing around the edges of his lips. 'But since it's you, my darling Caitlin, I don't think there's any danger of that.'

She gave a sigh of pleasure as she acknowledged his approval, and looked around the vast gallery space in Azraq which Kadir had commissioned to mount her debut photographic exhibition. At first she'd been worried that such a move might be seen as nepotism, but then a prestigious visiting dealer had seen it and asked if she would consider transferring it to London's Mayfair. There was even talk of turning it into a touring exhibition, for the Xulhabian Tourist Board were eager to show the world a different side of the country which had been so faithfully recorded by their young Queen.

Blown up and magnified were images from their honeymoon—almost two years ago now. Dramatic sunrises, star-spangled skies and a desert tortoise basking in the sand, beneath the shade of a *baswa* tree. There were arty shots taken around the palace, showing areas which the public never usually got to see. Much interest had been generated by her early portrait of Kadir, walking through the wide marble corridors with his robes flowing around him and, seemingly, the weight of his destiny hanging heavy on his shoulders. Yet the most recent photo was of him and Cameron on their horses, looking into each other's eyes and laughing. It showed a different side of the desert Sheikh—the more *human* side, as the international press were fond of putting it.

But pride of place went to a candid study of their son, holding the hamster previously known as Hamish. To Cameron's delight, the much-loved pet had been flown from Cronarty to Xulhabi, and then surprised them all by producing a litter of seven pups. And so Hamish had been renamed Hasina and her offspring had all been found caring homes.

Even Morag had found her own happy ending, for she had quietly married Ghassan, the head groom, in a simple and loving ceremony which would have melted the most indifferent heart. The middle-aged couple had been given their own small section of the royal palace and the Scottish nanny was able to continue to help care for Cameron—the little boy and future king who was thriving with each day that passed.

Caitlin sighed as she looked up at her husband. Her beloved husband who was now her greatest friend and advocate. 'I have you to thank for letting me show my work here, my darling,' she said softly.

'And I have you to thank for bringing so much light and love into my world and transforming it completely. And although I can never thank you enough, my flame-haired temptress, I can but try.' His black eyes glinted as his voice dipped into a provocative whisper. 'Maybe we should go home right now so that I can demonstrate exactly what I mean.'

Caitlin expelled a slow breath of excitement. Whoever would have thought that an illegitimate girl from Cronarty would have ended up thinking of a palace as her home? But she did. Yet she knew that if the world changed tomorrow and she had to go and live with Kadir and Cameron in that small croft on Cronarty—which they sometimes visited, unannounced—they would be just as happy. Because life wasn't about jewels and palaces, or ruling a huge country. It was about the relationships you had with the people around you—and hers were just the best.

When they got back to the palace, they would retire to their beautiful sandalwood-scented suite and undress each other at leisure. Her fingers would explore the honed muscle beneath Kadir's satin skin and he would make her gasp as he put his sensual lips to good use. She would enjoy his body—and he hers—as they'd done every time they'd made love. Which had been a dizzying and spectacular amount of times.

And later, when she was lying satisfied and replete in the warm circle of his arms, she would announce her news. Actually, she would make sure that most of the lamps were still lit, because she wanted to see his face when she told him he was going to be a father again. She wanted to capture his joy and keep it in her mind for ever, fixed there as permanently as any photograph. This time he would see her carry their unborn child and this time he would watch her giving birth.

A ripple of gratitude flickered over her skin as she nodded her head in reply to his question.

'Yes, my darling Kadir,' she murmured. 'Let's go home.'

* * * * *